A Dixie Christmas

...

Holiday Stories from the South's Best Writers

...

Edited by
CHARLINE R. MCCORD
and
JUDY H. TUCKER

Preface by
FRED CHAPPELL

Illustrated by
WYATT WATERS

Published by
ALGONQUIN BOOKS OF CHAPEL HILL
Post Office Box 2225
Chapel Hill, North Carolina 27515-2225

a division of
WORKMAN PUBLISHING
708 Broadway
New York, New York 10003

Printed in China.
Published simultaneously in Canada by Thomas Allen & Son Limited.
Design by Anne Winslow.

Library of Congress Cataloging-in-Publication Data
A Dixie Christmas : holiday stories from the South's best writers / edited by Charline
R. McCord and Judy H. Tucker ; preface by Fred Chappell ; illustrated by Wyatt
Waters.— 1st ed.
    p. cm.
  ISBN-13: 978-1-56512-483-7
  ISBN-10: 1-56512-483-9
  1. Christmas stories, American.   2. Christmas—Southern States—Fiction.
3. Short stories, American—Southern States.   4. Southern States—Social life and
customs.   I. McCord, Charline R.   II. Tucker, Judy H.
PS648.C45D59 2005
813'.0108334—dc22   2005045247

10   9   8   7   6   5   4   3   2   1
First Edition

Contents

Preface

by Fred Chappell

THE DAY'S OUTING WITH the Otter had been exciting but also tiring and now Mole and Rat were making their way home again and they put aside their apprehensions about villages with human beings in them and took the straight way through. Rat reassured his friend: "At this season of the year they're all safe indoors by this time, sitting around the fire; men, women, and children, dogs and cats and all."

And so they chose the broad lane and Kenneth Grahame describes their passage in these terms:

> The rapid nightfall of mid-December had quite beset the little village as they approached it on soft feet over a first thin fall of powdery snow. Little was visible but squares of a dusky orange-red on either side of the street, where the firelight or lamplight of each cottage overflowed through the casements into the dark world without. Most of the low latticed windows were innocent of blinds, and to the lookers-in from outside, the inmates, gathered round the tea-table, absorbed in handiwork, or talking with laughter and gesture, had each

that . . . natural grace which goes with perfect unconscious-ness of observation. Moving at will from one theatre to an-other, the two spectators, so far from home themselves, had something of wistfulness in their eyes as they watched a cat be-ing stroked, a sleepy child picked up and huddled off to bed, or a tired man stretch and knock out his pipe on the end of a smouldering log.

The Wind in the Willows is one of my favorite books, and "Dolce Domum," its fifth chapter, one of my favorite therein. Here Grahame presents, with the reassuring gracefulness of modesty, two major themes of his book: coziness as against danger and discomfort, in-clusion as against apartness.

Coziness is also a major theme of our American Christmas sea-son. Merchandisers depend upon our seasonal hankering for co-ziness and attempt to turn that yearning into a seasonal greediness. A kitschy nostalgia for Victorian Christmases that never existed in-forms our relentless commercialism. Many of us respond, perhaps more readily than we realize, to the sentimental greeting cards, the overdressed living-room tree, the merry harness bells of the Bud-weiser Clydesdales.

We respond to these images of well-lighted comfort because we know about discomfort. We are aware of those who, like policemen and firemen, find Christmastime a season of special peril. We know that a patient cleaning crew will appear after hours to clear away the mess of the Christmas office party. We know that a distant accompaniment to our jolly carols will be the lamentation of ambulance sirens and that while we sleep all snug in our beds hundreds of weary soldiers are guarding ammunition depots in lands where Christmas is not generally celebrated.

We know these things because these duties, or duties similar to these, have also fallen to us. The women and men who prepare the food for the church supper, who set up the tables and fuss over the flower arrangements, are cheerful in their tasks, but they hold that their true Christmas comes later, when they arrive in their own kitchens around midnight and pour a cup of tea and muse upon the tenor of the evening. They made the supper celebration possible; they were the essential part of it—and yet they were not part of it. The business at hand prevented their losing themselves in the general gaiety, though of course they enjoyed looking on. And now they sit alone in a ragged bathrobe at the kitchen table and sip the steaming mug and listen to the refrigerator hum and the furnace sigh and the stillness of the surrounding neighborhood.

It is a deep and vivid emotion but difficult to describe, this feeling of aloneness in the midst of the feast. We are not being excluded; we know that we may take our places at the table at any time. But just now during this particular moment, we are not part of the clamorous ceremonies, and individuality closes in upon us and holds us rapt in an obscure reverie where we seem not quite to belong to the world around us. Like Rat and Mole, we seem to be looking into Christmas as from outside a window and though the holiday mood appears to be at its happiest peak, its aspect seems strange to us, maybe a little alien.

Nor are we alone in our aloneness. We realize that others—maybe most others—come also to these moments of intense self-awareness and that they too experience this passage of melancholy divorcement. The thought may occur that Christmas is a thing too good for us, that we are adequate for everyday usages but lack the full measure of character that joy demands. And so we retreat a little into ourselves and pluck at the frayed threads of the bathrobe and wonder if we are deserving of the occasion. Everyone is sent an invitation to Christmas, but isn't it possible that ours arrived in the mailbox by accident, that it was intended for someone more deserving than ourselves?

IN THE MOUNTAINS of western North Carolina winters can turn dreadfully cold. I grew up on a farm in those hills and our water was supplied from a spring in a back-pasture holler by means of a pipeline we had laid ourselves. We had failed to dig the trench sufficiently deep and almost every winter the pipes froze in the earth and we had to dig them up, hacking at the brick-hard soil with rusty axes as well as mattocks and pickaxes. We disinterred the pipes and laid them on bonfires set at intervals along the trench line. The three-quarter-inch iron pipes would sing in agony before discharging bolts of ice out either end of a length. The three or four or five of us would laugh half hysterically when the ice let go. It was an exhausting business.

And it seemed to happen every year on Christmas Day or Christmas Eve. This can't have been an accurate impression, but it was the one we held, my father and uncle and the farm workers and my shivering self, too young to be of much help in the task. Yet we felt there was a crazy justice in the fact that the pipes froze and we had to labor in the merciless wind to chop them out of the ground. We felt, obscurely, that this was part of the price we paid for Christmas. Suppose the pipes didn't freeze; suppose the whiteface heifer didn't wiggle through the lot gate and have to be chased for hours over the rocky roads and through the muddy ditches; suppose Aunt Dinnie in her cabin near the end of the road didn't choose this day to fall prey to one of her spells and have to be spirited to the hospital and fretted over till the Christmas pot roast melted to a flavorful, tarry paste — how would one ever appreciate the comfort and coziness of the blessed day if its prelude consisted only of pleasant hours? But if you were attuned to hear it, the raw wind that poured off the slopes of Chambers Mountain bore the ghostly, silvery chatter of bells. It was good to be out on the steep hillside stabbing at icy dirt; it was a fitting preparation for the comfort of the Warm Morning coal heater and the mug of Russian tea that swarmed the olfactory nerves like a spice shop.

Now that water would come coughing rustily back into the house, we could have tea and coffee and my father and grandfather would have chasers for the holiday toddy that they enjoyed punctually once a year. *Best of all things is water,* says the ancient ode of Pindar, and it goes on to say that after water, gold is next best. My father claimed that the poet chose gold for second place because bourbon hadn't been invented yet.

But coffee belonged to the future and now we were still punching futilely at the frozen soil and methodically cursing our fates. Our hearts were not in our maledictions, though. This was our time of apartness from Christmas, a moment of aloneness that was, in quaint paradox, communal. The only way to speak about it—when we dared to speak about it—was in joking terms. I believe it was Roy John Ballew who said, "You know, if I wake up tomorrow morning and it ain't Christmas, I aim to hunker in and sleep till it comes around next year." And Junior Baucom said, "If I wake up and it ain't Christmas, I'm going to come out here and dig up them pipes so they'll freeze again. Them freezing is what brings on Christmas every time."

Perhaps some cultural anthropologist observing our situation would identify it as a vestigial purification ritual in which we scrubbed clean our souls in preparation for the sacred feast. But the pipes *were* frozen and my mother and grandmother grumbled and threatened. "How do you expect us to cook without water?" And an observing scientist would find that the language in our ritual phrases was decidedly unreligious. But maybe the notion this fictional anthropologist would form is not entirely fanciful. We felt ourselves to be different persons after the water flowed and the long joints were fitted together again and fresh, unfrozen earth was brought from the barn and sheds and heaped over the trench. I felt different from before and I could see from the half-grinning faces and straightened postures that the others did too.

Roy John lit a Camel and said to my father, "Well, J. T., that ought to hold it till Santy Claus shows up. Maybe your missus will give you a special present for getting this water to the house."

"Maybe she will," my father replied. "Or maybe I'll give her a special present first."

"Maybe you could both do it at the same time." But then Roy John reflected that he might have spoken too suggestively and looked away northward to hide his shyness.

"Can't have too much Christmas," my father said and then he told the other two men Thank you, it was mighty kind of you-all to help us out again, and he slipped each of them a twenty-dollar bill to buy, he suggested, a little stripe candy for the younguns.

They all shook hands, but my youth excluded me from this part of the ritual and our friends departed. My father and I stood unmoving for long minutes, watching the glow of Roy John's cigarette as it went bobbing along the roadway in the gloaming, seeming to move without human agency, like an escaped Christmas tree light that signaled a promiseful message.

My father shouldered a mattock and a shovel and I carried the battered old ax as we headed for the house. "We'll have to wash up with cold water," he said, "but won't it feel good to have clean hands again?"

• • •

So, I shall propose that the ordeal with the water pipes was indeed our purification ritual. With our hands washed and our hair combed and the gray-blond shadow scraped from my father's broad face, we were ready for the supper table with its hot biscuits, mashed sweet potatoes with butter streaming in rivulets, fried chicken, green beans my grandmother had canned, and for the adults gallons of sweet, black coffee and for my little sister and me — Russian tea.

In many places in America we still observe the ancient, customary habit of bringing into our Christmas companionship those who have exposed themselves to the darkness and the cold for our sake. We stand attentive to them, and after they have paid the ceremonial respects, we offer them our best good cheer and, if they so desire, the warmth and shelter of the house. These petitioners are, of course, Christmas carolers, and they are our neighbors and we recognize them gladly with their red noses and snow-bearing headgear. They sing, a little uncertainly and handsomely out of tune, "God Rest Ye Merry, Gentlemen."

It was a quite different troupe of carolers who came to greet Rat and Mole after they reached home safely and had taken a little something to eat and drink. The singers that came to visit our small, furry pals were field mice.

It was a pretty sight, and a seasonable one, that met their eyes when they flung the door open. In the fore-court, lit by the dim rays of a horn lantern, some eight or ten little fieldmice stood in a semicircle, red worsted comforters round their throats, their fore-paws thrust deep into their pockets, their feet jigging for warmth. With bright beady eyes they glanced shyly at each other, sniggering a little, sniffing and applying coat-sleeves a good deal. As the door opened, one of the elder ones that carried the lantern was just saying, "Now then, one, two, three!" and forthwith their shrill little voices uprose on the air, singing one of the old-time carols that their fore-fathers composed in fields that were fallow and held by frost, or when snow-bound in chimney corners, and handed down to be sung in the miry street to lamp-lit windows at Yuletime.

> *Villagers all, this frosty tide,*
> *Let your doors swing open wide,*
> *Though wind may follow, and snow beside,*
> *Yet draw us in by your fire to bide;*
> *Joy shall be yours in the morning!*

Introduction

THE STORIES IN THIS collection were e-mailed and snail-mailed, FedExed and UPSed, left in mailboxes, tossed on front porches, and left propped up against unsuspecting garage doors. Finding and experiencing each story, regardless of its packaging or mode of delivery, was like being the undeserving recipient of a gift involving great sacrifice, a gift unselfishly bestowed by one intent on stretching well beyond the comfort of his or her means to offer only their absolute best.

For the best kinds of gifts are words — spoken or written. The right words in the right order at the right time will always exercise a magical charm over their recipient. Long after the festive decorations have been returned to the attic, the mountains of unwrapped boxes have been dragged curbside, and the unadorned tree has been hauled off for recycling, the words of these stories — unaltered by time, undiminished by brevity of event — will continue to enrich their readers.

When the rush of the holidays is over and at last it is time to build a fire, reach for the last fruitcake cookie, and pick up *A Dixie Christmas*, we hope this small volume adds a coda to your holidays and brings you a few hours of serenity.

This year's collection opens with Marianne Gingher's "The Yellow Rose," which invites the reader to observe a family Christmas through the watchful eyes of a little girl. Steve Yarbrough delivers an unforgettable love story that melds the culture of the Mississippi Delta with that of Eastern Europe—bluegrass meets grand opera, bacon and grits mix with Hungarian stew. For an existentialist Christmas, read George Singleton's "The Opposite of Zero." No one writing today uses and controls the absurd as well as Singleton.

"In the Bleak Midwinter," by Georgia's Bailey White, describes a widower's insistent search for companionship. Jim Wade's got a thing for antique fans, while Ethel, the object of his affection, is on a mission to find a hot little woodstove. In "A Southern Christmas," an uncharacteristically sentimental Ellen Gilchrist records a childhood memory of a time when the world was at war and "the spirit of Christmas was very powerful."

Aaron Gwyn depicts a man at a crossroads in "The Road to Tarshish" when Leroy Crider's extended detour eventually brings him face-to-face with the ghost of what might have been. Rick Bass, a Texan now removed to the vast open spaces of the Northwest, draws a montage of a Montana Christmas replete with family tradition: a joyful children's Christmas pageant and a hunt for the perfect tree in the deep snow of a mountainside. Meanwhile, in "Buy for Me the Rain," a story of exquisite delicacy, Bret Anthony Johnston explores the many painful layers of loss. Central to Lynne Barrett's story "Gift Wrap" is a family recipe for lebkuchen—"love cookie" in translation, and therein lies a tale. In a personal essay, "That Clapton Christmas," Michael Parker reveals how the gift of music eased a twelve-year-old boy's passage from childhood to adolescence. And, finally, the book closes with Stephen Marion's "Old Christmas," in which a miracle of grace is bestowed upon a bunch of hard-luck boys in a jailyard.

Yes, it is true that these stories traveled to the reader by many different routes, all delivered to a common destination by random modes of transport. Their more important journey, however, is a tour of the regions of the human heart, both joyful and melancholy.

Christmas, with all its bright promises, could not shield us from heartache when we learned of Larry Brown's untimely death on November 24, 2004, just as we began hopeful preparations for the holiday season. His passing cast a deep shadow over the holidays for his family, his friends, his legion of fans, his hometown of Oxford, and his native state of Mississippi. Many of you will remember his excellent story "Merry Christmas, Scotty," the finale of our 2004 book. Who could have known when we positioned him at the exit of *Christmas in the South* and printed his cheerful closing—"Merry Christmas, everybody"—that so soon we would be offering a tribute to his quiet memory and his distinguished writing career?

Yet quiet memories are the essence of Christmas. We hope these stories, told in the fine and unmistakable style of our Southern writers, bound up and wrapped as a gift by the illustrations of Wyatt Waters, bring you peace, love, joy, and quiet reflection.

Waters, like the authors of these stories, is heir to the creative Southern genius. He sees with a clear vision deep beneath the surface, down to the very bone of a thing, and then portrays its complexity in vivid color.

The illustrations, as well as the writings in this volume, are the best the South has to offer you this bright and hopeful holiday season. Merry Christmas, Larry Brown. Merry Christmas, reader. Merry Christmas to all of us.

—*Charline R. McCord and Judy H. Tucker*

A Dixie Christmas

The Yellow Rose

by Marianne Gingher

Every evening, arriving home from his office or the hospital, my father swooped my mother into his arms and softened her up with a kiss. She'd grown prickly in the desert of his absence, tending us children all day. It was a juicy, watering hole of a kiss—you could hear it from any room in our house. He had a wide, plush mouth and no shame whatsoever, and he might have gobbled my mother right up where she stood cooking french fries or mashing potatoes had there been no small children underfoot, tugging at his pants leg, pulling his stethoscope out of his pocket, making whatever racket we could to gain access, to peel them apart. We could not have been more intrusive had we been skunks.

My parents had met in Dallas, Texas, in November 1945, and the story handed down to us kids was that Mother had been so immediately smitten that she came in from their blind date, summoned all her roommates to bear witness, announced that she'd met the man she would marry, then stood on her head. On their second date my father proposed to her, and less than three months later they married—the day after Valentine's, 1946.

From my child's perspective, a bold, compulsive, publicly demonstrative passion distinguished my parents' marriage. Certainly romantic urgency had been at the heart of their courtship and wedding; but even after we children began to crowd and pester them, they never lost center stage with each other.

They went out to parties often. They took weekend vacations without us — to golfing resorts mostly. They attended dinner dances, my father fretfully attired in a tuxedo, the bib and tie and cummerbund of which gave him such trouble that my mother always intervened. That he relied upon her to finish dressing him, to uncomplicate whatever he bungled or didn't understand, gave her an aura of competence that we children relied upon. He was the worker in the family, but Mother was the fixer, the mechanic and fine finisher. She stood by his side, matchlessly serene, wearing her emerald taffeta strapless evening gown, a sheath as slender as a blade of grass. She'd corralled three children for early baths, cooked and fed us supper, untangled our father from his tuxedo, and emerged from such tumult and squalor without one hair askew, without a wrinkle in the chic green gown.

I loved my mother in a needy, starveling's way. My brothers did too. We couldn't get enough of her. We competed with one another for her attention, and we competed with our father. We begrudged her long conversations with friends on the telephone. We'd lie on the bed beside her, twitchy with impatience, eavesdropping in plain view, waiting for her to hang up. It seemed we were stuck, unable to fully dramatize our lives without her approving audience. We depended on her spark, her ease, her companionable laughter, the compassion in her soft brown gaze. I swooned after the fragrances that trailed her: Lustre-Creme shampoo, Moon Drops cold cream, Jergens almond-scented hand lotion, the ornate, operatic bouquet of L'Air du Temps perfume. The latticework of those smells clung to the fabric of her nightgown along with the chirpy aroma of the bacon she fried us every morning, the secretive singed smell of her Chesterfield cigarettes mingling with the sweet cool vapor of her Doublemint breath.

She was everybody's friend and confidante, her heart a repository, a haven for the messy, complex matters of our childhood. She was an ardent listener. She thought we were all much funnier than we were. She savored our naive philosophies and responded with thoughtful and sober attention. She endured our follies and exploits, indulged our swagger with unwavering fascination, burying her mind in our evolution like a student rapt in deciphering illuminated manuscripts.

At no time was my mother more exalted than at Christmas. Our whole family scrambled around her like elves, trying to please. She was fun to please because she expressed her gratitude so flamboyantly. She could take a child's little molehill gift and, lifting it from its box, transform it into Mount Everest.

Ritually, the last gift she opened on Christmas Day was our father's. Too ostentatious to have been set under the tree (it would have made the other presents look shabby), he fetched it with much fanfare from the attic or a closet. The gift tended to be something my father couldn't easily afford, wrapped thickly in Montaldo's signature holiday papers, either dazzling metallic red or green. The bow seemed the truest prize, so artfully posh that I saved it and draped it around my neck to wear as a medallion days afterward.

Beneath their flashing wrappings, the Montaldo's boxes were a slippery dolphin gray, deep enough to hold whole ensembles of clothes. Traditionally, when she glimpsed their gorgeous and surprising contents, my mother collapsed into tears. It wasn't Christmas unless she cried. She lifted the silky garments from their bassinets of tissue into the light of Christmas Day with an expression of trembling reverence. She nuzzled them, inhaled their worldly fragrances, waltzed them around the room as the tears spilled down her cheeks. We children gathered around, stroking her. "Don't cry, Mommy," we implored. But there was something magical and inspiring about tears overflowing the wellspring of delight. The revelation that happiness had a mature and tender side—the opposite from ticklish and silly—expanded our repertoire. To watch our mother smiling through her tears was to witness the sort of paradox that inclined us to believe powerfully in the ultimate triumph of gladness over sorrow.

Once Daddy gave her a little squirrel stole; another year, a dress designed by Molly Parnis, who outfitted Mamie Eisenhower. One Christmas he gave her an emerald-cut diamond on a silver, thread-thin chain, and there was the morning she opened the smoke-colored beaver jacket and cried over it for nearly an hour. Each gift was impeccably tasteful—the salesladies at Montaldo's took Daddy carefully under their wings. They were the sorts of gifts my mother would have never lavished upon herself. Her own father had been a cheapskate. She recalled that during the Great Depression she'd owned two school dresses, a pink one and a green one, which she alternated from day to day. It's conceivable that my mother wept when she opened Daddy's grandiose boxes because her luck had so overwhelmingly changed. Perhaps she cried for all the women still living with cheapskates. How had she managed to attach herself to such a generous man?

I tried to imagine a gift that would make me cry, but I couldn't. Maybe a horse. Was it because we children were accustomed to generosity and had never done without? Because of her stingy up-bringing, my mother didn't take largesse for granted.

My father bumbled around in front of her tears. "Don't you *like* the dress, Bunny?" he'd say, perplexed. She'd laugh as she blotted her eyes. "I *love* the dress, Rod. You know I do. But it's too much. All I gave you was a boring old shirt." And her observance of the inequity usually triggered a fresh onslaught of tears. My father's reward was in knowing that he was the champion giver of gifts. It was his immutable status within our family.

Maybe his extravagance made my mother feel too much like a child, her ability to reciprocate in kind, dwarfed. Perhaps, in some way she couldn't articulate, my father's gifts made her feel beholden. How might she live up to his queenly expectations of her?

He thought he was being appropriately worshipful. He courted her anew with the packages she opened. There was a ruitualistic dance they performed of hesitancy and disapproval. Why had he spent so much? Why did Christmas turn him into such a boy? No matter how vigorous her protests, she couldn't shrink his capacious heart. If he stood mildly by, looking dumbfounded long enough, she'd rise above her uncertainties and chastisements and sink herself against him in an embrace that proved she was the happiest woman in the world.

THERE CAME A TIME, however, when she was not so happy. Daddy's practice was thriving, and perhaps she no longer felt part of the struggle they'd shared when he first opened his office in a rented ramshackle frame house with a dirt parking lot on Price Street. Now my mother was housebound, anchored by babies. She complained bitterly whenever Daddy played golf on his day off and stayed at the clubhouse for a cocktail that would make him late to dinner. When he finally arrived, she'd remove his plate from the warming oven, plunk it in front of him, and hasten with strident silence out of the kitchen. The food, overheated, looked like rigor mortis had set in. "Daddy's in the doghouse," he'd say, glimpsing me peeking at him shyly from the threshold.

He was seldom at home in the evenings. If he wasn't on call for emergencies, he went back to his office to update his charts. Assiduous about detailing patient histories, and because his secretary couldn't keep up with the drawling volume of his dictations, he tended to the task himself.

My mother was bound to have felt threatened by the allure of my father's work. It was not simply a career or a calling to him, it was a complete and satisfying seduction, a consummation. Did he seem too satisfied apart from her? There began too about this time, a parade of new cars, symbols not only of his economic advancement but also of his boyishly extreme enjoyment of that status. What he regarded as entitlement, or as reward for his hard work, my mother viewed as indulgence, as spendthriftery. My grandfathers had always paid cash for their cars, but my father didn't mind sinking flashily into debt. It would remain the pattern of a lifetime, his bringing home a new car every two or three years. Usually he would select a Buick or a Chevrolet—although there was a smattering of Plymouths. The smallest car he ever bought was a Valiant, and the largest, a true luxury car, was an Electra with innovative electric windows and locks. The Electra filled our little driveway like a docked cruise ship, and after my mother saw it, she didn't speak to my father for a week. She could get so feisty over a new car gleaming outside, awaiting her inspection, that she looked hot to the touch. "But we don't *need* a new car," she'd seethe. She would rather have had decent furniture for the living room, new rugs, a trip to New York City to see *The King and I*.

One night, late, I thought I heard my parents arguing. Daddy had returned from the hospital after we children were in bed, but I had never fallen asleep. Some nights when I felt restless, I'd trampoline on my bed for a while and practice flipping somersaults. The voices I heard bore no resemblance to those of my parents. They sounded shrill, desperate, and panic-stricken, like the shouting of people on a leaking ship.

"You're not being reasonable," the man said. "Where would you go?"

"To Mother's," the woman replied. "I'll take the children, and we'll go to Mother's." The firmness of her decisiveness troubled me. Her voice sounded eerily tearless. But the argument boomed from the den where my mother watched her melodramas, and so I reassured myself that what I'd overheard was the overwrought dialogue of actors on TV, not my parents.

Not long afterward, sitting at the kitchen table and eating lunch with her, I caught my mother moping. She looked dulled by disappointment, the expression on her face distinctly drifting toward sadness. She drummed her fingernails on the tabletop while she stared past me out the window into a thinness of expectations. She didn't *see* anything; when a car passed, her eyes didn't follow it. I tried to make conversation. "Why are all the songs on the radio about love?" I asked.

"Are they?"

"Yes. Isn't it dumb?"

"What else should songs be about?" she said, dragging herself out of her trance. "What else is more important?" Her voice turned sharp and defensive and as freighted with lament as the actors I'd heard arguing.

IT WAS DURING this palpable phase of my mother's displeasure with my father, her playing proctor to his bad boy, that I embarked upon my plan to be the person that Christmas who would give her the single present that would make her cry. Clearly my father had lost favor. I was not the perfect daughter by a long stretch, but I'd never let a clubhouse cocktail come between me and dinner, nor had I foisted upon her an unwanted automobile.

I must have been around nine years old, still too young to ride a city bus downtown to shop by myself. I remember Grandmother Ruth accompanying me to buy Mother's gift at Ellis-Stone department store on Elm Street. I wore my good winter coat over a dress and my white cotton church gloves. Those were the days when proper Southern ladies dressed up to shop downtown. My grandmother wore a prim gray suit, fashionable pumps with stout heels (not the spike heels my mother was fond of), a gray hat with a fluff of veil, and pearl earbobs. Christmas decorations entwined every streetlamp. Salvation Army bells unfurled sparkles of sound upon the chilly air; I pretended it was music shaken loose from a reindeer's harness. I felt like skipping across the crosswalks, but my grandmother clamped my hand firmly in her own, and we marched along to her stern, protective beat.

Ellis-Stone was the store where Mother bought our shoes. The shoe department operated a fluoroscope machine where you could see ghoulish green X-rays of your spindly toe bones inside new shoes and determine if you had a proper fit. Near the cashier's counter, a mechanical palomino horse outfitted with soft grimy leather reins stood ready to buck you around for a dime. I wanted to patronize Ellis-Stone not only because my mother approved of shopping there, but because it was where I'd seen the tiara. I'd determined to buy my mother a rhinestone tiara for Christmas because she was the queen and because I knew she'd let me borrow it whenever I felt like dressing up. It was a splendid crown of jewels, almost holy, like a halo. Whenever I played Monopoly and landed on LUXURY TAX, I thought of the tiara.

I'd told my taciturn grandmother about the tiara, and she'd agreed to escort me downtown to buy it; she'd offered neither an opinion nor enthusiasm. I believed that she secretly wanted the tiara for herself and was jealous that I'd planned to give it to Mother. At heart Grandmother Ruth was a Victorian, a former one-room-schoolhouse teacher, a knuckle rapper, a prohibitionist, humorless and bossy. She sulked if you beat her at card games. My mother dyed her hair the lively honey blonde of our cocker spaniel and she smoked cigarettes. She'd been an airline stewardess when she met and impetuously married my father. She was fond of saying—and didn't mind if Grandmother overheard—that if she hadn't fallen in love with Daddy her ambition had been to sing torch songs in nightclubs.

I tugged loose from my grandmother's grip, scampered across an expanse of snow-colored marble, and entered Ellis-Stone through a heavy glass door. I made a beeline for the glass jewelry case where I'd seen the tiara. Alas, the beautiful crown of wishing stars had ascended, levitated from its earthly perch on black velvet and floated away to make somebody else's dreams come true. "Sold," the saleslady confirmed, and although she showed me a simpler, child-size version, I remained nearly inconsolable. It seemed as if the entire fate of the world had shifted dramatically, as it would have had there been no wise men bearing their precious, inimitable gifts.

Grandmother Ruth was quick to point out an array of pins constructed of rhinestones: the prettiest was shaped like a snowflake. But I knew that my mother wasn't a pin person, nor a bracelet person for that matter. Bracelets would manacle her busy hands and get in the way when she did dishes. Pins were sedate old lady jewelry. Fairy-tale queens and princesses wore crowns and necklaces and glass slippers, not pins. Perhaps in pointing them out my grandmother was thinking of something *she'd* like for Christmas.

"Could I interest you in pearls?" inquired the saleslady.

I shook my head vehemently. Only rhinestones would do. Then I saw the necklace. I hadn't noticed it, because it was out of the case, draping the neck of a plastic torso. Rhinestones dribbled in all directions, bejeweling the mannequin's collarbones. There were three strands of rhinestones from which dangled larger pear-shaped stones. The effect was that of an elaborate constellation caught in a spider's web. "That's the one," I said.

The saleslady hesitated. "It's very showy," she said, glancing at my grandmother for reinforcement. "Does the lady you're buying this for go to evening parties? Dances?"

"Often enough," said my grandmother tersely. I could tell that she thought the saleslady was being nosy.

The saleslady began to unfasten the necklace from the display. I observed what a complicated process it was because the delicate separate strands kept tangling. Finally she arranged the necklace on a bed of cotton inside a flat white box and gift wrapped it. "That will be $2.98," she said. It was all the money I had in the world.

Afterward, to celebrate, Grandmother Ruth took me to the S&W Cafeteria and allowed me to eat two chocolate puddings for dessert and the sugar-loaded orange drink (instead of milk) that my mother never bought me. Howard Waynick, who was a neighbor of my grandmother's, played the organ there on the balcony above the lobby. As soon as we'd eaten lunch, we walked over to speak to Howard and my grandmother requested "Winter Wonderland," which Howard played jauntily. He gave me his autograph on a napkin.

On Christmas Eve, my father left work early to shop. He had a few traditions of his own that he didn't rely upon my mother to sustain. He bought a couple of cartons of fresh eggnog at the grocery. He bought a few fifths of Jack Daniel's whiskey at the ABC store to distribute to some of his doctor friends. If a patient hadn't already given him a fruitcake, he went out and obtained one. It was food nobody in our family would eat except Daddy. Even new fruitcake looked old and leftover. The petrified fruit was as hard as marbles. Daddy said there was a trick to eating it. If you dunked it in eggnog, it was delicious, he said, and we were all really missing something if we didn't try it. Fruitcake looked like a loaf of baked dog food to me.

Off he went on his secret errands, which included a ritual stop at Montaldo's on Christmas Eve, mind you, without a clue in his head about what Mother wanted. He preferred giving gifts that hadn't been requested, that were total surprises, that nobody would have thought to ask for. He relied on the taste of the matronly staff and on his weak judgment of what Mother would look good wearing, or the sorts of clothes he'd like to see her wearing—which tended toward the provocative: low necklines, slits in skirts. He liked showing her off. Fortunately the majority of clothing sold in Montaldo's in the early 1950s tended to be decorous and prim, what a rich pilgrim on the cutting edge of fashion might have worn.

This particular Christmas Eve he motioned me aside and asked if I'd accompany him. The invitation was an astonishing breach in tradition. Nobody was supposed to know what Mother's gift was until she opened it. "We'll listen to Christmas carols on the radio," he cajoled. "Come on, Punky, ride with me so I won't be lonesome."

I should have guessed that he was charting new, uncertain territory on this trip. We didn't drive in the direction of Montaldo's at all. We stopped instead at Harvey West Music Company, and I followed him inside to the record department. "I'd like to buy a copy of 'The Yellow Rose of Texas,'" he told the clerk, but they'd sold out.

We left and drove to Moore Music Store, then to a place in south Greensboro near Hamburger Square, where the bums slept under newspapers. I wasn't allowed to go with my friends to the National Theater in south Greensboro, even though we all hankered to. They showed only horror movies there, and the black people in the balcony, which was where they were required to sit, poured soft drinks and popcorn on the people below—at least this was the rumor.

I liked strolling down the sidewalk in south Greensboro with my tall, cheerful father. It wasn't the menacing place I'd been told it was at all. Between the parking lot and the store where we were headed, my father ran into at least three patients and enjoyed friendly conversations. By the time we arrived at the music store, it seemed like an incidental stop. They didn't have one copy of "The Yellow Rose of Texas" in the place.

"Maybe we ought to give up," I suggested.

"Oh, we'll find it somewhere," he said, marching up the street toward Woolworth's. Snow flurried around us. I remember thinking that his perseverance had something to do with the snowflakes spinning miraculously down from the sky. We never had a white Christmas, but suddenly there was the possibility of one. We loped north on Elm Street toward less seedy shops. We couldn't get half a block without my father running into somebody he knew. Shaking hands he seemed taller and gladder than anyone. His birthday was February 12th, Abe Lincoln's birthday, and striding along beside him I could believe my father was somebody famous too. He was the embodiment of robust goodwill, and I felt its warm contagion, keeping company with him on the street. I felt on the verge of reward. And finally in Woolworth's we located a single 45-rpm recording of Mitch Miller's rendition of "The Yellow Rose of Texas" that we'd first heard on *Your Hit Parade*.

"Don't we have to shop for a record player now, so she'll be able to play it?" I asked him after he'd paid for the record. It cost ninety-seven cents. My parents didn't own a record player, but he shrugged.

"I'm not buying it for her to play," my father said.

Of course he'd never mentioned during our excursion that he was shopping for Mother. Why had I assumed it? He was the one who admired "The Yellow Rose of Texas," not Mother. He loved all up-tempo ballad-type songs, rousing gospel, Sousa marches, alma maters, themes from popular movies, and cowboy tunes, music that glorified bravery and sentiment. Whenever "The Yellow Rose of Texas" played on the radio, he'd tap his foot to its beat and grin and tell my mother that it was *their* song, that she was his yellow rose. What was she to do with such a cornball? She'd flip the dial on the radio, dousing his sentimentality with the sophisticated music she preferred: Rosemary Clooney, Judy Garland, Dinah Shore, Frank Sinatra, Perry Como, Julius LaRosa, Nat King Cole.

The pioneer spirit was very much the rage then. My brothers had asked Santa to bring them Davy Crockett coonskin caps. James Arness had premiered as Matt Dillon in television's first adult western, *Gunsmoke*. John Wayne was a leading box office star. "Cattle Call," sung by Eddie Arnold, was a hit single, along with Mitch Miller's "Yellow Rose of Texas."

But my mother wasn't a cowgirl. She didn't sing along with "The Yellow Rose of Texas" like she sang along with Patti Page crooning the "Tennessee Waltz." She liked wistful, heartbroken tunes. If Daddy thought this record was the sort of gift that would make her weep with joy, I figured he'd set himself up for disappointment—if indeed the record was for her. It didn't seem at all like my father to spend Christmas Eve shopping for himself. What did it mean, if he was giving her a record that she couldn't play? It meant a lucky break for me and my fabulous rhinestone necklace. Clearly I'd won our competition, and riding along in our warm car on Christmas Eve, my father whistling with larky confidence, victorious in his purchase, I felt a little sorry for him.

ON CHRISTMAS MORNING everybody in our family— except Grandmother Ruth and Granddaddy—ate breakfast in their pajamas. We didn't even bother to comb our hair. It was Grandmother Ruth who insisted that, after breakfast, teeth had to be brushed, beds made, dishes done, before the first present could be opened. Of course we all howled with protest—even Daddy.

Our ritual for opening presents was to gather around the Christmas tree and wait for Daddy to read the tags, one at a time. When your name was called, you opened your present while everyone watched. You passed the present around to be examined and exclaimed over. Nobody dove in and opened their loot in a rush. It was a slow, methodical, infuriating process of observation, mostly. The slowest gifts were the ones Daddy opened from patients: boring gifts like golf tees or highball glasses. There was the occasional adult gift with a private joke behind it, given by some wisecracking friend, like the set of pillowcases my mother opened one year. On one side of each pillowcase was a little rabbit wearing a sombrero; embroidered beneath him was YES. On the other side of the pillowcase, the rabbit was lying down and snoozing under his sombrero and the word embroidered under him was NO. My mother and father laughed and winked at each other and tucked the pillowcases back in the box before my grandparents could ask to see them.

That Christmas my parents gave me a record player and the records I'd asked for: *The Nutcracker, Peter and the Wolf,* and the *Peer Gynt Suite*— suggestions from my piano teacher, Mrs. Lake. I also received a Ginny doll, a baton, and several Nancy Drew mysteries. There were the obligatory clothes from grandparents: a new flannel nightgown, bedroom shoes, a crinoline, a fancy church dress. The pile beneath the tree began to dwindle.

My brothers opened football helmets and shoulder pads, two puzzles, Lincoln Logs, cap guns, Mickey Mouse watches, and coonskin caps. My father received mostly socks and shirts and ties. I was reduced, after buying my mother's necklace, to giving him a box of Chiclets. No matter; he acted thrilled, and he slid them into his bathrobe pocket as if to suggest that he would want to chew one soon so would keep them close at hand. My grandparents opened a dull assortment of blankets and towel sets, a new toaster. There were interruptive phone calls all morning — from distant aunts and uncles and my grandparents who lived in Illinois — that waylaid our progress, and by noon, when every kid in the neighborhood was already outside testing a new bike or Flexible Flyer or roller skates, our opening ritual began to feel like a chore. Friends would phone, incredulous that we weren't finished opening. "You're not done? You're kidding! It's one o'clock!" And on we labored, fortified by cups of eggnog that Daddy poured.

Finally only two presents remained under the tree; a flat parcel containing "The Yellow Rose of Texas" and my gift, wrapped expertly in silver with a blue bow by the professional Ellis-Stone gift-wrapping department. "Why don't you open Marianne's next," Daddy suggested. "'For Mommy,'" he said, reading the card.

"What lovely paper," my mother said appreciatively. I stood close to her, watching her fingers gently split the taped seams of the paper. My heart felt zithery, anticipating her delight. "What a nice sturdy box," she said with admiration as she carefully lifted the lid. On a pristine bed of cotton, in a glittering tangle, lay the necklace. No telling how many times my brother Knothead had shaken the box, trying to guess what was inside it. "Oh my goodness gracious!" exclaimed my mother.

"You can't even tell what it is until I untangle it," I told her.

"But of course I know what it is!" she said. "It's the sun and the moon and the entire Milky Way all in one. It's jewels fit for a king."

"A queen," I said. "It's to be worn only on special occasions."

"Well, then, let me put it on right now."

"It will make you look rich."

"I'm already rich," she said, pulling me into her arms. We fiddled with the necklace and got it straightened out. I fastened it around her neck, even though she was still wearing her frumpy bathrobe. "How do I look?"

"Beautiful," everyone cooed, and my mother hugged me close and kissed me and told me over and over how much she loved the necklace—but she didn't cry.

When she opened "The Yellow Rose of Texas," she cried. She held it for a long time, as if absorbing its tune and lyrics by telepathy. She rolled the record slowly between her hands, considerately, meditatively. I didn't know why such a gift would make her cry, didn't understand it's magical declaration. I only understood that my parents communicated on some level of intimacy that I would never be privy to.

"For goodness sake, it's Christmas Day!" Grandmother Ruth said. My mother's tears embarrassed her. "What a mess," she said, bustling out of her chair to gather up the torn paper leavings of our celebration. She could never sit still for long; she was like a human pogo stick.

"Not just yet, Mother," my father said to her, "there's one more gift." Then he took my mother's hands and led her to the entrance hall closet where a new mahogany hi-fi stood gleaming. Inside its cabinet were stacked a half-dozen record albums by popular musicians my mother admired. And although she was thrilled with the gift and sang its praises and kissed my father over and over, I saw that the gift didn't equal the little corny record he'd given her earlier, the record which dismantled whatever fences over the past months my mother had thrown up to part herself from him. And he was right; she never played "The Yellow Rose." It was a keepsake, a souvenir that she tucked away. I never saw it again, but it played indelibly in the air, inaudible, inexhaustible, all the days of their lives.

IN TIME I would learn that the necklace I'd given my mother was gaudy, not her style at all, a cheap floozy's adornment. My mother and I would reminisce about the gift and what a tender little girl I'd been and how she'd treasured the necklace in spite of the fact that she never wore it in public. One time, for my sake, she pretended to. That same holiday, on the evening of the Century Club Christmas dance, accompanied by my father trussed up in his tuxedo, my mother left wearing her strapless green ball gown and the twinkling rhinestone necklace. Her neck and shoulders looked wreathed in a galaxy of light. I stood waving good-bye at the window. I never knew, until I was grown, that after she settled herself inside the dark car, she carefully removed the necklace and replaced it with her wedding pearls.

In my mind, the necklace had transformed my mother. I was watching the ascent of a star. All the men would line up to dance with her. Their wives would covet the necklace and beg to borrow it. My parents would drink champagne out of glass slippers, and when they danced, all eyes would be cast admiringly upon them. Hero and heroine of a true-life love story, they would float above the dance floor, airborne, dream borne, far above the mortal and the picayune.

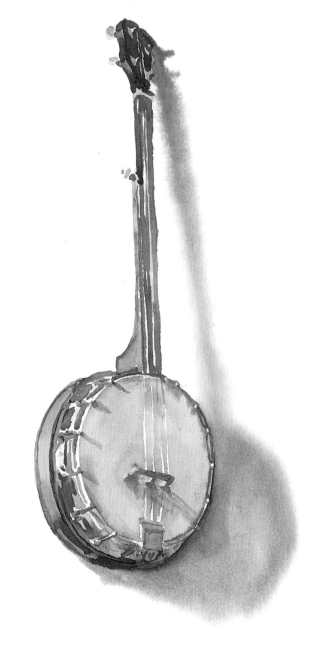

Hungarian Stew

by Steve Yarbrough

Malina is dreaming about a particular bench in Lazienki Park, a bench where she often sits and reads on warm summer afternoons while Petita, her cocker spaniel, prowls the pathways, looking for an unsuspecting cat. She's been going to that bench for more than fifteen years. The first time she went there she was a student new to Warsaw — thrilled to live in the city of Chopin and Prus, pleased to be away from her parents and her grandmother. The last time she sat on the bench she had just left the Victoria Hotel, where the airline has its offices, and there was a round-trip ticket to the U.S. in her purse. She stayed a long time that day, wondering if she would ever see Lazienki again, wondering if a year from now she'd want to.

Suddenly she feels a finger poking her in the ribs.

"Hey," Jack says. "Wake up. You're about to miss Delta Implement Company."

There's bluegrass on the car stereo, a fast song Jack loves: "Foggy Mountain Breakdown" or maybe it's "Rocky Top." A shower of banjo notes washes over her. She sits up and looks out the window. Through the darkness she can see a bunch of tractors rowed up in a lot beside the highway.

She rubs her eyes. "What time is it?"

"Ten till one. Welcome to Indianola, Mississippi, home of B. B. King and me."

She and Jack have driven straight through from western Virginia. She thinks she fell asleep in Memphis.

Driving through town she sees a McDonald's, a Kentucky Fried Chicken, something called Mr. Quik that looks a lot like a 7-Eleven. She's been in the country for only six months, but she's already learned that in America all small towns look alike, at least to a foreigner. She wonders if that's true of Poland too.

Jack turns onto a narrow street. The houses here are small and perfectly square. Chalk animals stand before a couple of them. In one yard she sees a pink flamingo. Christmas lights ring picture windows, tinsel hangs from trees glittering behind plate glass.

Jack parks at the edge of a driveway. They get out and walk across the yard toward the house. It's dark, but as they near the door a porch light comes on.

Jack's father opens the door. He's a huge man, even larger than Jack. He has wavy gray hair and a red face. He's wearing a pair of glasses and a terry cloth bathrobe. In his right hand he holds what looks like a Luger. Porch light plays on the barrel.

He slips the pistol into the pocket of his robe and offers his hand to Jack. "Hey, son," he says. "How you been doing?"

Jack shakes his hand. "Fine," he says. "Good to see you."

Then Mr. Westbrook looks at her. "Good evening," he says, smiling broadly. "We sure are glad you come off down here to see us."

His accent is thicker than Jack's. For a moment she's afraid she won't be able to understand him. People from Mississippi have a love affair with vowels: they never seem willing to let them go.

"Hi," she says. "Was that a Luger you were holding?"

She can tell that he's impressed. "Sure is," he says. "I haggled with an old boy five years before he let me have it. Had to blackmail him even then. You interested in handguns?"

"Not really. But my father had one like that. He took it off a German officer during the Warsaw Uprising."

Mr. Westbrook laughs. "You won't have to worry about no Germans down here," he says. "We've got a lot of riffraff, though. The town's seen three killings in the last year alone. Folks just open up the door and get shot."

He leads them into the living room. Jack's mother and grandmother are waiting up. They're both small gray-haired women, indistinguishable, really, from each other. They both hug her. Then his grandmother—whose name is Annie—says she has to return to bed.

"I left my electric blanket on," she says, "and I hate to throw money away. If you ask me, electricity's a wasteful discovery."

Jack has told Malina that his grandmother still has every pair of shoes she's owned since the Great Depression. He says she and his grandfather, who died only last year, almost starved in 1930; she has never believed in her modest prosperity. It's a kind of behavior Malina thinks she understands. Every year as September approaches, her own grandmother begins to store food in preparation for a German offensive.

Thinking of her grandmother makes her edgy. It's two days before Christmas. This time last year she and Adam were riding the express train to Olsztyn. This year, she knows, Adam plans to go alone. Two days from now, on Christmas Eve, she'll phone. She'll have to talk to her husband and her mother and her grandmother, wish them all a Merry Christmas, and do her best to evade questions about when she's coming home. Her exchange program takes an academic year, she will say. The academic year ends in May.

"Y'all must be hungry," Jack's mother, Darlene, is saying. "You want bacon and eggs or a sandwich?"

Jack pats his stomach. "Bacon and eggs," he says, "and I wouldn't mind some grits on the side."

Malina offers to help in the kitchen, but Darlene says she must be tired and orders her to rest. So she sits down on the couch in the wood-paneled den and listens to Jack and his father.

"Your grandmother," Mr. Westbrook says, "she's slipping fast, son." He glances at the door to the hallway to make sure it's closed. "She's pinching pennies like never before, and she's convinced there's nothing ahead but disaster. She finally found a good deal on a monument for Henry, one of them his-and-hers markers, and they told her it'd be cheapest if she had as much of the engraving done right off as she could. So we go down there the other day to see it, and it's the damnedest thing. On her side it says, Annie L. Pope. Born May 3, 1910. Died—and there's a blank spot followed by a one and a nine. I looked at it and I said, 'Annie, what are you aiming to do if you live past the year 2000?' She gets this surprised look on her face like she hadn't entertained that possibility. 'Well,' she says, 'I just can't afford to do that.'"

Jack and his father laugh, and Malina joins in. But at the same time, she thinks of the last talk she had with her grandmother, the week before she left for the U.S. "The next time you see me," her grandmother assured her, "I'll be stretched out under a slab on the hill above the lake. But I love that little lake. My husband and all my friends are buried there. There's no better place in the world to be dead."

She and Jack eat a huge greasy Southern meal, during which Jack frequently praises his mother's cooking. Darlene beams as each forkful disappears into his mouth.

Tomorrow, Jack promises, Malina will prepare Hungarian stew for dinner; it's his favorite of all the dishes she's cooked for him during the last three months. He says you have to taste it to believe it.

She's shown to a bedroom across the hall from the one where Jack will sleep. Jack waits until they're alone in the hallway and embraces her.

Resting her cheek against the front of his shirt, she inhales his odor. The way he smells is one of many things she loves about him. He says it's the soap he uses, Irish Spring, combined with Brazilia, his cologne. The other night he proposed they put them together and market a new scent. They would call it Atlantic Crossing.

Now he says, "I'm so glad you came with me. I didn't think you'd agree to do it."

"I didn't think I would either," she says. "I just didn't want to miss the chance to spend Christmas with you."

"Maybe we'll spend other Christmases together."

"Maybe," she says.

He squeezes her tightly. "Good night," he says. "Get some sleep."

She wakes before dawn feeling nauseated. Every item on her plate was soaked in Crisco. She already knows they'll expect her to eat the same type of food again at breakfast, so she makes up her mind to stay in bed late.

JACK WORKS FOR a newspaper in Roanoke, Virginia. Malina met him at Virginia Tech, when he came to give a talk at the School of Communications. The title of his lecture was "The Development of Newspapers in the Deep South." She saw it advertised in the student paper and decided to attend. She wanted to learn as much about the country as she could, and she had a lot of empty hours to fill.

She can't remember much about the lecture. What she remembers is how hot the night was. It was the heat that led her to drink so much punch at the reception, and it was the punch that made her head foggy.

She found herself standing in a corner. She had stood in a lot of corners lately. A few American graduate students had invited her to parties, but when she got there she had a hard time talking with them. They never became more than a group of moving mouths, of gesturing hands and confident smiles. They kept breaking up into components — big white teeth, long pink nails.

That night at the reception she noticed that Jack was standing in a corner too. She'd seen a few people shake his hand right after the lecture, but from then on everybody ignored him. He kept refilling his cup, just like she did, and staring at the floor with a forced grin on his face. She'd begun to think Americans never felt uncomfortable; she was grateful to him for showing her that wasn't the case. She drained her cup, walked over to him, and told him she'd enjoyed his talk.

He laughed. "Doesn't look like anybody else did. I saw a couple of people nodding off."

"I thought it was really informative."

"Hell, I hope it was," he said. "I'm not exactly academic. I spent most of last night digging through the *Encyclopedia of Southern Culture*, trying to come up with something to say. Problem was, I kept getting sidetracked. I read all the entries on blues and country music, and then I got off into the section on Southern cooking. I'm from Mississippi," he said, "and I like to eat."

He wasn't fat, but he did have a belly. It strained at the fabric of his navy blue sweater.

She said, "Well, you sounded knowledgeable."

"If you don't mind my asking," he said, "where are you from?"

"Poland."

"I bet you like Szczypiorski."

None of her professors in the English department had heard of any Polish writers except Milosz and Herbert. She said, "How do you know about Szczypiorski?"

"I've always been interested in Holocaust novels," he said. "I read

The Beautiful Mrs. Seidenman last year, and it knocked me out. I've got another one of his books at home, but I haven't read it yet."

She said, "I live in Warsaw, and I often see Szczypiorski drinking coffee and eating cheesecake at the Telimena Café." She loved to sit there herself, read a paper, and sip tea. She had not known how much she'd miss those daily pleasures.

"Next time you run across Szczypiorski," Jack said, "I wish you'd buy him a drink and tell him there's a guy in Virginia that thinks he's hot stuff."

She laughed. "Oh, I don't think I could do that. I don't know him personally."

He said she was probably right not to do it. In Boston a few years ago, he told her, he'd phoned his favorite American writer—it was someone she'd never even heard of—and asked if he could take him to dinner. The writer said yes. At the restaurant he was princely, but a few weeks later, when Jack called to tell him how much he liked his newest novel, he sounded delirious. "He kept saying, 'Sue me if you want to,'" Jack said, "and then he started crying. I finally hung up on him. That was my last contact with celebrity."

He looked around the room, then glanced at his watch. "I guess I've done my bit for American education. You want to go out and grab a drink?"

Evidently he had not noticed her ring. She wanted to go with him, wanted to sit in a bar with an American man and find out what that felt like, but she didn't know what it would mean if she did. She said, "I've got an early class tomorrow. Maybe I should say no."

"Listen," he said, "do you have any idea what's happening right now, not more than six blocks from where we stand?"

"No."

"The Bluegrass Cardinals are in town."

"What are Bluegrass Cardinals?"

"Just a bunch of country boys with enough money to buy themselves some leisure suits and some nice guitars and banjos. In other words, a bluegrass band. A really good one."

"I've got a lot of Wordsworth to read," she said. "*The Prelude.*"

"Just imagine what your friends back in Warsaw'll say when they find out you had a chance to witness a whole performance by the Bluegrass Cardinals and passed it up for a prelude."

The bar was dark and smoky. On either side of the bandstand stood a massive totem pole. Most of the men in the room wore blue jeans and boots, plaid shirts, and cowboy hats. The women had long lashes, and their hair was stacked up high.

The band was good, the music fast and intricate. But the song lyrics were sentimental, and the lead singer sang them so seriously—eyes squeezed shut, a flutter in his voice—that she burst out laughing once or twice.

She and Jack sat in a booth at the rear of the room and drank one beer after another. They talked between songs and during the intermission. He asked her a string of questions—about her job, her apartment, Warsaw, Solidarity, Tyminski, Walesa, and Polish vodka. He said he'd read a lot of books set in Poland, and he'd love to see the country one day.

"And I've read Faulkner," she said. "I'd like to see Mississippi."

While they talked, she kept waiting for his face to break up. But despite all the beer some adhesive held him together. I am looking at a person, she told herself. This man, this American, is an entity of substance, a thing of mass and feelings.

She wondered what he saw when he saw her. Did he think she had lived her whole life in a cage, that she'd spent entire days roaming the street looking for something to eat? Would it stun him to discover that she owned a lot of books, a German car, half of a cottage on the Baltic coast, and that none of those possessions meant any more to her than they might have to him? Her heart pumped blood just like his did.

They kissed in the parking lot. He exuded a tropical odor.

"You know what?" she whispered. "I'm married. I should have told you."

"I saw your ring," he said. "I'm lonely. That's what I should have told you."

"You didn't need to. I figured it out."

Somebody drove by in a pickup truck and whistled.

He said, "I wish you'd come home with me."

"I want to," she said, "but my husband would never do this to me. If I go home with you, I'll feel horrible in the morning."

"I had hoped," he said, stroking her hair, "that we could put off the morning for a while."

. . .

SHE SAW HIM almost daily but resisted moving in.

His house clung to a mountainside halfway between Blacksburg and Roanoke. When the wind blew, the branches of trees scraped the roof. At midnight a train rumbled by a few hundred feet below. He said it was the New River train, made famous in a bluegrass song.

"That's why I bought the house," he said.

The house had four bedrooms, two baths, a basement with a big woodstove. Every fifteen or twenty seconds, when you were taking a shower, the water would stop. It was something to do with a lack of pressure in the pump.

"I got the place cheap," he said, "because one day it'll slide down the mountain. By then I'll be gone."

"Gone where?"

"Mississippi."

"You want to move back?"

"Sure," he said. "It's home."

He was thirty-five and unmarried. His relationships with women, he said, tended to end badly. The only woman he'd ever lived with had left him because he refused to feed her goats. He made a decent salary but spent most of it on records and books. He ate dinner at places like Bonanza and Wendy's. He never separated his clothes into colors when he washed them, so a given shirt might change hues three times in two weeks.

"It's the sartorial equivalent of recycling," he said.

He lay beside her for hours, kissing her hair, kissing her eyes, her fingers. He made her name her body parts in Polish.

They took long Sunday drives on the Blue Ridge Parkway. He'd vacationed in the mountains with his family. He pointed out a motel where they'd spent a night in 1963.

The mountains in autumn were burnt orange and gold. Mornings were cold, but by noon the sun had burned the chill away. They lay on a blanket in a meadow near Galax, listening to old-time fiddlers. She loved a tune named "Soldier's Joy." It had come from some war, Jack was uncertain which.

He had never played chase among ruins, he did not know what treasures a bombed-out building offered. He had never worn unlined shoes to school through ankle-deep snow. His father had not disappeared in the fifties and returned with a limp and a lisp. Clicks and pops when he talked on the phone were not unnerving.

She had married her best friend. More than half her history was inseparable from his. He could finish singing any song she could start; he couldn't start a song she couldn't finish. She knew before he did when he wanted to leave the party. She could tell from the way he handled certain objects—ashtrays, coffee cups, keys—when something she had done was displeasing. If she came home late, he knew where she had been, which friend she had gone to visit. "How's Nina?" he would say. "Did she get her sink fixed?"

Too much of her life had been like that. She knew the other actors' moves and moods, she knew where all the props were. She knew when the lights would dim. She knew all her lines, and delivering them on cue was an easy thing to do. But every performance sapped a little more of her interest in the role.

This is it, she thought as she lay beside Jack in bed, the mountainside rumbling from the motion on the rails. *Real life is really beginning.*

She could swear she heard a banjo playing somewhere.

ANNIE, JACK'S GRANDMOTHER, is standing in the kitchen, looking at the small Polish cookbook that lies open on the countertop. Malina stuck the book in her bags as an afterthought the morning she left Warsaw.

Annie wrinkles her nose. "I can't make out none of this," she says. "I thought I'd be able to recognize a word here and there."

"I'll translate for you," Malina says. "The recipe calls for one and a half pounds of pork with bones, three tablespoons flour, one medium onion, two and a half tablespoons of fat for frying, five cups of sauerkraut, salt, ground paprika, one bay leaf, and red wine."

"Wine?"

Too late Malina remembers that Annie is a staunch Baptist. According to Jack, she considers fermentation a diabolical process. "You just add a splash of the wine," she says.

"I've lived eighty-one years," Annie says, "without soaking up a single drop of alcohol."

It's starting to go badly, Malina thinks. She wishes Jack were here. He's out back with his father, looking at a new riding lawn mower. Why anyone would want to ride a lawn mower is beyond her. Darlene has gone Christmas shopping.

"A little wine," Malina says, "is good for the circulation."

Annie says, "You aim to keep circulating with Jackie?"

Malina doesn't know what to say. For obvious reasons, Jack hasn't told them that she's married.

"He wants everybody to think he likes living off up yonder in that house all alone, but that's really not true," Annie says. "When he was down here last Christmas, he told me, 'Grandma, I'm lonesome.'"

Jack did not see his family last Christmas—he had to work—but the fact that Annie would lie to help secure his happiness makes Malina want to embrace her.

"I know that boy well," Annie says. "I think he wants to marry you. I bet he'd like to have babies."

She imagines her features melded with Jack's. She hears thin little voices crying *Mamusia*, sees herself sitting in a rosewood rocker, nursing one baby after another. Adam has never wanted children. Whenever she brings up the subject, he has to take out the garbage or change the car oil.

She wipes her hands on the apron she's wearing. Her eyes have grown misty. She says, "I like Jack a lot, Annie. He'd make a wonderful father."

Annie puts her arm around her. Malina feels the frailness in her bones. "Don't you worry, Marlene," Annie says. "I'll eat your stew, alcohol and all."

While Malina prepares the meal, Annie hovers nearby peppering her with questions about her family. Malina tells her that her father died five years ago, that her mother is healthy—she still works as a clerk in a bank—and her grandmother lives alone in a one-room apartment in a city not far from the Lithuanian border.

"She was born in Warsaw," Malina says, chopping up the onion on a cutting board, "but she moved away after the Second World War." She remembers the way her grandmother's voice crackles when she speaks about the basement she and Malina's mother lived in during the worst of the bombing. The only working stove was on the third floor; she had to risk her life to boil milk. "She left," Malina says, "because she didn't think they'd ever rebuild the city."

"That war messed Indianola up too," Annie says. "They tore down four nice houses so they could build an ugly armory. Spent a whole wad of money putting the thing up, and soon as they drove the last nail in, the darned war ended." She shakes her head. Clearly the waste still disturbs her.

They eat dinner at a big table in the dining room. On a hutch nearby stand several pictures Malina first noticed last night. Jack at age six, dressed up like a cowboy, with fringe on his cuffs and shoulders. A graduation picture in which he's wearing cap and gown, and a picture of him in his football uniform. He's the only child Darlene and Mr. Westbrook had, the only living creature they can cling to in old age.

Having only one person to hold on to, she thinks, must be a frightening prospect. She comes from a sizable family, has two sisters and a brother, a bunch of nieces and nephews. Three or four times a year they get together.

Forks flashing, knives clattering against their plates, the Westbrooks and Annie agree that Malina is a great cook. Darlene says, "What all's in this stew?"

Before Malina can reply Annie says, "It's mostly stuff that you wouldn't think would fit together." She spears a piece of pork, as if to punctuate her statement. "A little of this and a little of that, but you mix it all up and it's nothing but nice."

Darlene says, "I want to get the recipe before y'all leave." She ducks her head girlishly and says, "Of course, I hope you'll come back."

Malina says, "I want to."

Want isn't *will*, and from the way Jack stares at his plate, she can tell he noted the verb choice.

Annie lifts her napkin, dabs her mouth, and says, "Marlene, honey, what part of Poland is Hungary in?"

SHE AND JACK and Mr. Westbrook are in a pickup truck on their way to the liquor store. The Luger is under the seat. It's Christmas Eve morning, and Mr. Westbrook has said that tonight, after his wife and mother-in-law are in bed, they'll all share a drink. He wants Malina to taste Wild Turkey.

Sometime this afternoon she'll have to phone Poland. By tonight, she thinks, she'll need a good drink. She's spoken to Adam only twice since she started seeing Jack. Both times he sounded worried, as if he feared that something was wrong but had no idea what. His letters betray the same concern. The other day he wrote,

I can't wait until May. By the way, you haven't told us yet what day you'll be home. Doesn't an open ticket need to be revalidated? Don't forget to do that in advance. He wrote those words at the desk in their bedroom, a small unfinished pine desk that they waited in line one cold morning to buy. They chose everything in their apartment together. All the items they own reflect consensus.

Mr. Westbrook drives them down the town's main street. Jack points out the Piggly Wiggly, the store where his mother buys her groceries; a Santa mannequin in the window turns from side to side. Silver bells dangle off the streetlights.

They make a left turn. Jack says, "There's the newspaper office." He jabs his finger at a building that looks like the shops you'd see in an American western: there's a big glass window with bold letters on it, an awning overhead. "The paper's called the *Enterprise-Tocsin*," Jack says. "It's good, but it could be better."

"I've been trying to talk Jack into buying it," Mr. Westbrook says.

Jack says, "With what?"

"There's plenty of folks here that'd still loan you money."

Jack turns to her and laughs. "How'd you like to be a reporter-copy editor-typesetter-distribution manager-delivery person?"

"You'll have to let me think about that."

The liquor store is out on the highway. She and Jack wait in the pickup while Mr. Westbrook goes in to buy the whiskey. It's warm in the pickup even without the heater on. The people on the streets aren't wearing coats, just sweaters or Windbreakers. It's probably snowing now in Poland.

Jack takes her hand. Last night he came to her bedroom and sat beside her on the mattress. "That night I met you," he said, "I just wanted to take you to bed. I don't know what's happened. I ended up wanting more." He said he hoped bringing her here hadn't been a bad idea. She said it hadn't, she liked his family very much. But the truth is that Mississippi isn't Virginia, just as Hungary isn't Poland, and the house on the mountainside is too far away. For three months she's talked with almost no one but Jack. Now, suddenly, the rest of the world is back.

He says, "You look sad."

"I'm not sad," she says. "I just feel a little strange. This is the first Christmas I ever spent away from Poland."

"Are you thinking about your husband?"

"Do you want me to say I'm not?"

"It'd be odd if you weren't," he says. He looks out the window. Through the front of the store they can see his father. He's standing at the counter chatting with the man behind the register. Shelves filled with bottles line the walls. "You know, you've never really told me what Adam's like."

"He's a wonderful man," she says. She enumerates his fine points: he's honest, kind, hardworking, very bright. He's devoted to her. He would do almost anything she asked.

Jack tries a joke. "Sounds a lot like me."

"In some ways," she says, "I guess he is. Probably the biggest difference in Adam and you is that you've made me fall in love and he was never able to."

Mr. Westbrook comes out of the store with a brown bag under his arm. He gets in the truck and hands her the whiskey. "This stuff'll make you see double," he says. "But since I'm starting to lose my eyesight, I figure I can stand a little extra ocular power." For the first time she notices just how thick his lenses are.

On the way home he stops the truck near a green board fence. Through the spaces between the boards, she sees old cars piled up on one another. On a light pole, about twenty feet above the ground, rests a rusty red Volkswagen Beetle. A legend on one door says A&H USED PARTS.

Mr. Westbrook says, "That's nothing but the shell of the car on the pole. Every year or two they have to put another one up there. It rains a lot here, and old cars on poles rust out pretty quick."

He says the reason he stopped here has nothing to do with junked cars. "Back in the forties," he says, "this junkyard was used as a POW camp."

Jack says, "I didn't know that."

The camp never had more than ten or fifteen prisoners, Mr. Westbrook tells Malina. The camp commander hired them out to local farmers. He didn't worry much about escape, because there was nowhere the prisoners could go except Greenwood or Leland.

Mr. Westbrook says his father worked the POWs in his cotton fields. "The prisoners were German," he says, "and by and large a sullen bunch. One or two of 'em could speak a little English, but not much. Daddy used 'em to chop cotton along about July. There was one old boy that kept claiming he wasn't one of them. He swore up and down he was Polish. Said they took him prisoner and made him serve in the Wehrmacht. You ever hear of anything like that happening?"

"There were many instances of it," she says. "Mostly in the south and southwestern parts of Poland. There were many people of German origin in those areas who spoke Polish and considered themselves Polish, but the Germans didn't agree."

"Daddy always thought the boy was lying," Mr. Westbrook says, "but I couldn't help but believe he was telling the truth. The others didn't seem to have much use for him, and I figured that was a good sign." He shakes his head. "I can still remember the name of the place he said he was from—a town called Gliwice," he says, getting the pronunciation almost right. "Just saying that word made his voice break."

She can see him: a big Silesian boy in his early twenties with hair the color of straw. For all he knows, everyone he loves is dead. He leans on his hoe in sweltering heat, in a field six thousand miles from home. Mosquitoes buzz near his face. Slowly he pronounces the name of a place. The sound of the word is all he has left.

She feels as if a sock has been stuffed into her throat. "What happened to him?" she says.

"I don't know—they sent 'em someplace else," Mr. Westbrook says. He releases the clutch and pulls into the road. "But I've always liked to think that somehow he made it back to Gliwice."

• • •

After lunch she and Annie and Jack visit the cemetery. Annie intends to lay a plastic wreath on the grave of her husband. She has chosen plastic, Jack says, because it can be used again next year. She's a little bit worried that it might be stolen.

The cemetery looks just like the cemetery in Blacksburg. Most of the markers are small, and there are no slabs over the graves like there would be in Poland. The street runs close to the spot where Jack's grandfather lies.

They park the car and walk across the brown grass. Jack's grandfather's marker has two granite pillars. She notices the dates by Annie's name.

Annie leans over and places the wreath at the head of the grave. "He was an awfully good man," she tells Malina. "I'll be proud to lay next to him through eternity."

Jack puts one arm around Annie and another around Malina. "I wish Grandpa could have met you," he tells Malina.

"He sure would have liked her," says Annie.

For a moment they stand there, Malina bound to Annie by Jack. He has brought them together. A woman born in Mississippi in 1910 and a woman half a century younger from the Mazurian Lakes. She marvels at his power to pull her—even as, with one gentle motion, she begins to draw away.

She's standing at a small table in the den. Jack and his parents and Annie are lined up on the living room couch. The four of them talk quietly, the lights from the tree throwing various shades upon their faces. She can see them in there, she can hear their voices, but the sounds they're making refuse to form words.

She's holding the receiver close to her ear. The last five times she dialed, the call failed to go through.

She hears the long series of beeps that signal a successful attempt. The phone in her mother's apartment begins to ring.

Her grandmother, legs swollen and breath coming short, puts her hand to her mouth. Adam's fingertips whiten on the arms of his chair. Her mother is already there, lifting the receiver. There's a carol on the stereo. "Lulajze Jezuniu," Hush, Little Jesus. It's a badly scarred record, one she listened to as a child. She hears the old song clearly, even here in this new world.

"Malina," her mother says, "we've been waiting."

"I know," she says. "I have too."

"How are you?"

"I'm fine. How's Grandmother?"

Her mother hands her grandmother the phone. She hears the labored breathing. "Malina," her grandmother says, "I'm alive again at Christmas."

It's as if she's opened a gift box and found another year inside.

"I know you are," says Malina, "and I'm grateful."

"When will you come home? No, wait, Adam wants to hear you say it. He's having silly ideas."

When he comes on the phone, he sounds tentative. "Malina?"

She remembers an attic apartment in West Berlin. It belonged to a friend, who let them live there one summer when they were working illegally. At night they lay awake listening to a street singer who looked for all the world like Herzog's Stroszek. He played the accordion, and they always wanted to give him money, but the marks were what they had come for. She worked all day in an *eis bistro;* Adam made rolls in a bakery. They earned enough to buy a Volkswagen in decent condition, and they drove it all over Germany and into Belgium before it was time to go home.

Berlin is no longer divided, but she knows she is, knows that in some sense she always will be. There's a corner of herself she will have to wall off. For the most part she'll probably succeed. But someday, she thinks, some ordinary day, when she's loitering on a street in the Old Town, looking at French fashions through a shop window or admiring leather goods at a sidewalk bazaar, a sound will stop her heart. Wafting toward her on the breezes of a Warsaw autumn, as light as the fingers that pluck it, the tinkling music of a five-string banjo played in the Old Town Square.

The Opposite of Zero

by George Singleton

It took until seventh grade before I had—what I thought of initially as—an idiotic teacher call my name wrong on the roll at the first of the year. She got through Adams, Bobo, Davis, Dill, Farley—the easy ones: there were only easy last names in Gruel, no foreign names like Nguyen, Abdelnabi, Gutierrez, Haughey, Narasimhamurdhy, Papadopoulos, Napolitano, Xu, Yablonsky, Yanashita, Zhang, Zheng, Zhong—Goforth, James, Knox, LaRue, before she came upon my last name. Me, I came from a long line of utopians who pronounced our last name like the opposite of silence. Noyes, like "noise." My great-great-great-great something was John Humphrey Noyes, leader of the Oneida Community, a man who believed that God spoke to him, et cetera. Mrs. Latham went through her junior high class roll and when she came to me she said, "Gary No Yes?"

I said, "Maybe."

Of course I'd been in school with my classmates from kindergarten on, and they all yelled out, "No, Yes!" like that. "No, Yes! No, Yes!" They had never noticed the possible mispronunciation, but then again I hadn't either.

"Gary No Yes?" Mrs. Latham said. "Well. I bet you'll do quite well on true-false tests."

And that was it for me. No one ever called me Gary Noyes again. I took shit from that point on until my comrades started having sex, started telling me about how their dates kind of yelled out part of my name during intercourse — either "No, no, no, no," or "Yes, yes, yes, yes." Some of them — debutantes-to-be — went ahead and said my name in full, over and over.

It didn't matter that all of my other teachers pronounced my last name correctly from eighth grade onward, that even some of my philosophy, religion, and literature professors in college up in Chapel Hill had studied up on, and written about, my great-great-great-great whatever. Every one of my classmates called me Gary No Yes for the remainder of my time in Gruel. In French class they called me Non Oui. I changed over to Spanish and became No Si. Gruel Normal didn't teach Greek or Latin or German. These days I blame my lack of globe-trotting on the fact that I took only two first-year introductory courses in separate foreign languages.

Right after the original incident I came home and said to my mother, "There's a new teacher at Gruel Normal and she may or may not be stupid, Mom. She can't say our last name. She calls me No Yes. She thinks my name's Gary No Yes."

My mother's maiden name was Godshell, but that's another story.

"You must take 'farts' and turn them into 'rafts' to float away on, Gary," my mother said. "Your father will tell you the same thing.

He once told me that your great-great-great grandfather—or maybe your aunt—underwent a similar problem because of his ancestry. It makes us all stronger people. You must take 'shit' and turn it into 'hits.'"

My mother never said anything about turning lemons into lemonade, oddly. I could count on her to stay away from the clichés, and always wanted her to turn dirty words into aphorisms. After I became No Yes I would come home sometimes and say, "Patty Goforth said to me, 'Eat me now,'" only so I could see my mother drop her vacuum cleaner and rewire her brain to figure out what "eat me now" could turn into.

"Meant woe!" she would yell. "Patty Goforth is in some pain, Gary. What she's saying is, she's hurting. Probably from her home life. You need to be a lot nicer to her, what with the situation she's in."

My father said, more often than not, "I wish someone had called me No Yes when I was a kid. That's all right. *No Yes*. Ha! I think you're lucky to have Mrs. Latham for a teacher." Then he made us hold hands at the dinner table while he prayed for something like eighty minutes. My father had trickled down from being an Oneida plate maker into a man who sold specialized venetian blinds to people living in mobile homes. My mother—a Godshell—hailed from people in eastern Kentucky who thought anyone without a toolbox might as well be standing next to Satan.

Should anyone come up to me now and ask—let's reach way out and pretend a psychologist—"Do you think you come from a fine, hardworking, and moral family?" I'd say, without thinking twice, "No, Yes."

Mrs. Latham confused me daily. She claimed to use the Socratic method of teaching—which none of us figured out, seeing as she never explained Socrates—and later on I realized that she kind of misrepresented, or stretched, pedagogical terms. Maybe my memory's off, but I remember her saying more than once a week, "If Sparky walked ten miles north at five miles an hour, and Rufus walked five miles south at ten miles an hour, would they meet halfway in between?"

Lookit: my name might've been No Yes, but I fucking knew that it mattered where they started. Let's say if little Sparky began his wayward and unlikely hike in the Yukon Territory, and Rufus started in Pensacola, then Sparky'd be frozen and Rufus would drown. Who were Sparky and Rufus anyway? I thought. Was this the beginning of some kind of off-color, racist joke? Sometimes my father came home from a highly productive day of selling six-inch-wide venetian blinds and told my sister and me a joke about little Johnny ingesting BBs and later shooting the pet dog.

"No? Yes?" Mrs. Latham would prompt.

I wouldn't even raise my hand, thinking she called on me. I said, "Maybe," every time, without divulging my keen geographic knowledge.

"Miz Latham, I have a dog named Sparky," Alan Farley always said. "He's fast. He can go a lot faster than ten miles an hour, I know. He can chase a car all the way down to Old Old Greenville Road. My daddy dropped him off in Forty-Five one time, and he found his way home in less than an hour. Forty-Five's something like twenty miles away."

"No? Yes?"

Becky Herndon said, "I have an uncle named Rufus, but he keep saying he's going to change his name so no one doesn't think he's black."

I thought, each day, *You idiot, Becky.* I said, finally, "Sparky and Rufus need to find other ways to entertain themselves, ma'am. As many times as they walk north and south, they'll hit foreheads too many times."

"Exactly! Pretty soon they'll learn to walk east to west, right?"

I didn't get it. I wanted out. Every time Mrs. Latham asked us about Sparky and Rufus—and she was supposed to be teaching us English and U.S. history, not math—I came home and told my mother. I said, "Mom, Mrs. Latham keeps asking us about two guys walking toward each other. In the real world do people walk toward each other at different speeds every day? Is this something I need to know about? Yes or no?"

My mom always put down her dust mop, or can of Pledge, or Lysol, or prescription bottle of "special pills," or spatula, or can of Raid, or feather duster, or putty knife, or bottle of vodka "your father doesn't need to know about," or box of jigsaw puzzle pieces, and said, "There are many, many words that you can come up with for 'yes or no,' son. As in, 'Rosy One.' You can figure out the others. Right? Can't you?" Then usually she'd say, "Here comes your dad. Hey, don't say anything about the bottle of rubbing alcohol."

I would nod, then find my way to the push mower, even at dusk, even in winter. Usually I'd find my sister somewhere out in the back-yard, either gnawing bark off a sweet gum tree or burning insects with a magnifying glass. Judith was in the fifth grade, in my old elementary school wing at Gruel Normal, when I sat in Mrs. Latham's class. Judith had a destructive streak no one in our family could trace back in the gene pool, seeing as we came from those utopians.

Mrs. Latham must've really enjoyed her woodburning kit at home. Each year she made little personalized signs to go on her students' desks, kind of like nameplates used by CEOs, or professors who needed to remind colleagues that there was a Ph.D. at the end of their family names. Mrs. Latham handed these nameplates out on the last day before Christmas vacation—Mr. Adams, Miss Bobo, Misters Davis, Dill, and Farley, Miss Goforth, Miss James, Mr. Knox, Miss LaRue, Mr. Pendarvis, Mr. Pinson, Miss Seymour, and so on. They were perfect, on thin oak, and slid into specialized metal stand-up frames balanced at the front of our desks. Everyone else's was perfect— she didn't write out in cursive "Pin son" or "Go forth"—except for mine. There, in quarter-inch-deep brown letters, stood my name as she pronounced it.

I said, "What did I do? I didn't do anything," which wasn't quite true. Earlier that day I intentionally wrote down every wrong answer on a true-false test because I knew that John B. Dill—that's what he insisted on being called—copied from my paper. At the bottom of my test I wrote "Opposites" so Mrs. Latham would get it. Because it was Christmas, Mrs. Latham lobbed up some softballs, too: "Antarctica is the most populated continent." "The capital of the United States is Gruel." "Abraham Lincoln is best known for his tales of the Mississippi River."

"You let me know who's cheating on tests, and I want to thank you for it," Mrs. Latham said. "When you get your paper back after the break, I'll put a big fat zero at the top in case John B. Dill looks over your shoulder at it, but write 'opposite' above it. That's not what I want to talk to you about, though, Mr. No Yes."

Already I knew it was a trick. I tried to think of the opposite of zero. Was it one? Was it a hundred? Was it infinity? I said, "I need to get home pretty soon because my mom wants to go shopping up in Greenville," which wasn't true either.

Mrs. Latham sat down behind her desk. She shoved aside the gifts our parents had bought, wrapped, and handed over for us to give. Ten kids out of our class moaned, at eight-thirty that morning, when the first present happened to be a pencil holder. Mrs. Latham got so many wooden block pencil holders she could've built a cabin, as it ended up. John B. Dill's parents gave her a tie, for some reason. My father—bless his heart—gave her a gift certificate for specialized miniblinds, should she ever move out of her regular house into a trailer.

"The opposite of zero is yes, by the way—I can tell by the look on your face that you're trying to figure it all out. But that's not what I want to talk to you about, specifically, either. I want to talk to you about the two most powerful words in the English language. You might go to church and hear that those words are *good* and *evil*, or *love* and *God*, or—around here—*cotton* and *gun*. But the real answer happens to be *yes* and *no*. More has happened in the history of our land because of someone answering *yes* or *no* than any other two words, Gary. That's why I like to call you Mr. No Yes. I don't like to advertise it here in Gruel, but I took a bunch of philosophy courses in college—a load of courses about the existentialists. Yes and no were major themes in all of their treatises, which you—I hope and feel sure—will come to understand later on in life. Do you understand what I'm talking about?"

Another trick, I thought. Was I supposed to offer up one of the two most powerful words in the English language? I had no choice but to nod. I didn't want to let Mrs. Latham down here in the holiday season by saying, "Maybe."

"I would also like to tell you that sometimes in March or April the farmers have put their gardens in. They've planted tomatoes, beans, okra, squash, watermelon, and cucumbers to take over to the Forty-Five Farmers' Market. And out of nowhere a giant frost comes in for just one night. A lot of people think that it'll kill the plants, but a good gardener knows better. His plants become what is called 'frost-hardened' and they somehow become stronger. No one knows why, but frost-hardened plants can later withstand bugs and drought and too much rain. Even hail."

I said, "Yes, ma'am," like I knew where this was going. I didn't.

"And that's what I'm doing for you, Gary No Yes. I'm frost-hardening you. After you get out of my classroom, you're going to be so strong you'll be able to withstand anything that comes your way. I made a promise to someone years ago to act thusly. Do you understand what I'm talking about?"

I didn't nod this time. I said, slightly, "Yesnomaybe, uh-huh."

Mrs. Latham said, "Good." She said, "All right," and clapped her hands together. She wore a sweater with a Christmas tree on it, with two ornaments right about where her nipples would be, I thought. I tried not to look. I tried not to think about how I hadn't noticed this earlier in the day, maybe when we had to stand up and do jumping jacks beside our desks. "Now. For more important things. What's Santa Claus going to bring you? Your ma tells you all about Satan Claus, doesn't she? Oh—that's called a Freudian slip. I mean *Santa* Claus."

I stood up to go. "Well. I don't know. We don't make a big thing out of Christmas. Dad says we should celebrate the birth of Jesus more, and the birth of Sears, Roebuck less. I'd kind of like to get a new globe, a telescope, and maybe a set of encyclopedias."

Where did that come from?

In my eyes Mrs. Latham's Christmas ornaments shook up and down, though she didn't appear to laugh. She said, "I want to give you an extra credit question for your test. Yes or no: Mrs. Latham is stupid to believe in Santa Claus."

I looked behind her at the clock. Could it be that only ten minutes had passed, or had I been there for *twenty-four hours and ten minutes*? I imagined my friends already playing basketball down on the square—or our version of basketball, which meant hitting Colonel Dill's statue straight on the nose for two points—and my mother circling the den with a drink in one hand and a box of rat poison in the other, worrying that I had run away from home. I said, "Please don't do this to me. I can't take it any more. I don't mean to be disrespectful, ma'am."

Mrs. Latham got up from behind her desk and clicked her way toward me standing there. Her hair stood up on end in a way that spaghetti might look infused with static electricity. She put her right hand on the crown of my head. I might be wrong here—maybe she told me to scoot on off and have a wonderful holiday—but what I heard came out, "Wait till we get to Easter, No Yes."

I ran home without looking back, scared that a life-threatening disease had happened upon me. This was seventh grade, but it was the early 1970s, understand, and I had no prior reason ever to get an erection in Gruel, South Carolina.

My father wanted to invite my seventh grade teacher over for day-after-Christmas leftovers. He said, "We can straighten all of this out." He said, "We'll invite Mr. and Mrs. Latham over, and we can have turkey hash. We should've invited them over four months ago, as a matter of fact. Town like Gruel, we invite new-comers over. Did we bring them a pie or cake when they moved in? Hey, if there's one thing that I can understand from my ancestor John Humphrey Noyes, it's that forgiveness is next to godliness."

My mother, tilting in the den, said, "My dictionary has some words in between, which start with *f* or end with *damn*. But that's just me. That's just my personal dictionary. Listen. Like I said before, you can turn 'Latham' into 'halt Ma.' That's all I have to say. I can't believe that it didn't hit my brain earlier. That's all I need to say! That woman is damaging our son, I can tell. When have I been wrong?"

This occurred on Christmas Eve. My sister Judith huddled in the bathroom with a watercolor kit, as usual. Mom had encouraged her artwork, though only on the shower curtain where it would come off four times a day. Me, because I always woke up earliest, I discovered such dictums as "We shall never repent from our immoral ways!" or "It's a straight line between boredom and death!" or "May the Prince of Darkness teach us forever!" or "Roses are red / violets are blue / I've got a secret: / may the Prince of Darkness come out of nowhere in the middle of the day and select you for one of his minions." Judith wasn't right in the head, I figured out early on. This was before any of those scary movies, too. She'd get straightened out two years later, I thought, when Mrs. Latham called her Judith No Yes.

"Maybe you were wrong when we got married," I almost heard my father say. He looked up at my mother's secret cabinet, above the refrigerator. I do know that he said, "You thought I'd only be selling venetian blinds to convicts, ex-cons, runaways, and ne'er-do-wells. Look how that ended up. I seem to be putting food on the table. I don't hear you wanting for want."

My mother stomped around a bit, between running into various pieces of furniture in our den, living room, and kitchen. She asked me for a syllabus, kind of—she said, "Hey, Gary No Yes, get me that long sheet of paper that has y'all's day-to-day activities typed up on it, mimeographed with the goddamn teacher's name and address on the top of it"—and found Mrs. Latham's home phone number.

And she called. Only later in life did I find it sad that Mrs. Latham answered the phone, considering. Here it was, Christmas Eve, and she should've been either visiting her folks or her in-laws, like every other American with any sense of duty. I hung out by the stolen Christmas tree my father bought from a man on the side of Highway 25, and I pretended to be enamored with a couple of gifts wrapped for Judith and me which were obviously either socks or underwear. My mother said, "Hello, Mrs. Latham?"

I assumed that my teacher said something other than, "Get lost, it's Christmas Eve."

"Hey, this is Gary No Yes's mother, and I would like to invite you and Mr. Latham over for some day-after-Christmas turkey hash. I have this recipe I got from my mother's mother, and she got it from my husband's father's father's father's mother." I looked beneath the tree and saw a box that might've actually been a set of encyclopedias. "Yes, that *is* odd how my family could know my husband's family, but that's the way it goes. Anyway, we want you and Mr. Latham to come over on December 26th — it's so much trouble for people to take care of everything the day after Christmas, we understand."

I picked up a package and shook it. The card said "From Mom / To Gary." This is no lie: *glug, glug, glug* emanated beneath the box. Booze, I thought. It wasn't hard to figure out how my mother made it sound that she would bear the brunt of taking on all day-after-Christmas eaters. I listened to my mother listen to Mrs. Latham.

My mother said, "Uh-huh. Uh-huh. Okay. Uh-huh. Well, that would be great, then," like that.

To me she said, "Well, that's settled. She seems to love you, Gary No Yes." Back in the bedroom later I heard her tell my father, "She has no right to call herself Mrs. Latham. Halt Ma! She's not even married. What kind of a woman would pretend to have a husband? Most sane women walk around town with their husbands, but pretend like they're strangers who happen to walk in the same direction at the same pace."

The next thing I knew, my father got me out of bed, told me to put on some tennis shoes but stay in my pajamas, and we were off in his Dodge to place surprise Christmas gifts on the miniature porches of house trailers. He gave out extra-thin feather dusters, made especially for the Galloway micro-miniblind. Somewhere halfway to Forty-Five he said to me, "Gary No Yes, it's important to make people feel like their homes are first-rate. Remember that. Even if the homeowners aren't clean, it's important for them to feel that their trailers are first-rate. Am I clear on this?"

I thought, *We must turn "first-rate" into "rat strife." We must turn "first-rate" into "tar fister."* I said, "Yes," got out of the car, wove my way through about twenty curs, and propped micro-miniblind dusters against aluminum doors. I imagined my sister inside the bathroom, painting a picture of Santa Claus with horns and fangs.

THE *GLUG-GLUG-GLUG* GIFT ended up being a quart of aftershave, about enough to last the rest of my life if I ever started to use it at all. Judith got a new shower curtain, some more watercolors, a white leather Bible, and a slew of kneesocks. Me, I got underwear, some kneesocks that were probably meant for Judith and mispackaged, and one of those miniature black Magic Eight Balls that you shook to get a yes or no answer. I'm ashamed to admit it now, but when my father said, "Ask it a question and see what comes up," I secretly asked myself, "What does the future hold for me in regards to Gruel?"

I hadn't quite gotten the hang of how to ask it questions, obviously. The answer came up, *Outlook not so good.* I kind of thought how maybe Mrs. Latham came from the family that manufactured these things.

So we sat around the table for a few hours seeing as my father needed to pull off a two-hour grace, he couldn't carve the turkey right, and my mother kept throwing away entire cans of congealed cranberry sauce when they didn't slide out unmarred. "It's bad luck to have dented cranberry sauce," she said. "We must turn 'dented' into 'tended.'"

Fa-la-la-la-la, la-la, la-la.

My mother shaved, honed, scraped, and pulled what turkey carcass scraps she found soon thereafter, chopped the meat into dustmote-sized bits, set them in a pot of boiling turkey broth she'd saved, added enough jalapeños to cure the world of headcolds. The next day she got up earlier than usual, took the lid off her turkey hash, sampled a wooden spoonful, and declared, "One day I might open up a diner here in Gruel. What this town needs is a good diner."

I waited for my mother to turn one of her words into another, but she didn't. No, she seemed happy and confident and optimistic.

When Mrs. Latham came over at noon, my mother took off her apron, answered the door, and performed a perfect sweeping arm for my seventh grade teacher to follow into the den. Mrs. Latham said, "Merry belated Christmas, Mr. Noyes," to either my father or me, I couldn't tell. She didn't use the normal No Yes form of salutation.

"Judith, come on in here and meet Gary No Yes's teacher," my mother yelled out. I prayed that Mrs. Latham wouldn't have to go to the bathroom during her visit. Sure enough, Judith had taken her new watercolors and painted a nice representation of Grant Wood's *American Gothic*, but instead of a pitchfork the farmer held up only his middle finger, and the farmer's wife had blood running down both sides of her mouth.

Judith came out all smudged and said, "I guess you'll be my teacher in two years, if I don't fail on purpose. My last name's Noyes, not No Yes, by the way. You have from now until then to memorize it."

I said, "Ha-ha-ha-ha-ha-ha-ha. Judith got a new Bible for Christmas."

Mrs. Latham said, "If I'm here in two years you can go ahead and shoot me in the brain, Judith," as my father pulled the dining room chair out for her. "Did Santa bring you that set of encyclopedias you wanted, Gary No Yes?"

My mother pulled out her own chair and sat down. "How come you insist on people calling you *Mrs.* Latham when you don't even have a husband?"

My father said, "Dorothy Marie." I never knew my mother's middle name up to this point.

Judith said, "Marie? Marie!" and ran back into the bathroom to paint something else.

I said, "We are humbled by your presence here, Mrs. Latham," because I'd heard it in a movie.

My teacher scooted up. She looked at my mother and didn't blink. "My husband was in Special Forces. He was killed in 1968 somewhere in a Vietnamese jungle. I don't know about you, but where I come from we keep our deceased husband's name. We'd met in a college up in Chapel Hill, and I asked him not to volunteer, but he was too patriotic. His father and two uncles all died in France and Pearl Harbor. My husband had straight As right up until he left college his junior year. He studied philosophy and religion, and minored in literature. He had hopes of one day teaching elementary school either in an inner city, or way out in the country—kind of like here in Gruel—so kids could have some kind of future. My husband didn't so much believe in the war in Vietnam, though, let me make it clear. He thought that he'd studied enough Buddhism to talk the enemy into giving up altogether. He's buried down in Florence, at the national cemetery there, should y'all wish to ever visit and place a small American flag on his grave. The one I placed yesterday should be faded by the end of January or thereabouts."

My father stuck out his palms to hold Mrs. Latham's hand and mine before he said grace. I looked at my mother and noticed how

I could've taken every available linen napkin, wadded them up, and still not filled the space her open mouth created. My father only said, "Let us remember our heroes and victims. Amen."

Judith shouted from the bathroom, "Amen."

My mother let the canned cranberry sauce fall out at will, on a silver-plated stick-butter dish. She served the turkey hash atop cheese grits, with homemade bread to the side. Mrs. Latham finally said, "My husband had straight As just like Gary does. That's maybe why I'm a little hard on your son."

My parents said nothing. Even Judith knew not to say anything about how she wanted to be a tattoo artist later on in life. We ate, Mrs. Latham left, and my father and I spent the next week visiting his micro-miniblind customers to see if they'd tried out their surprise feather dusters. When I went back to school for the second semester, Mrs. Latham took me aside on the first day right before we filed off for a lunch of cling peaches, black-eyed peas, corn bread, steamed cabbage, and sloppy joes. She said, "Yes or no: That story I told your parents could've gotten me a movie award."

I looked into my teacher's eyes and realized that I would be getting such questions for the entirety of my life. I wore my sister's kneesocks that day, though no one could tell seeing as we didn't have a PE class at Gruel Normal. But I felt the smile coming on, and let it go before laughing out loud. I said, "Christmas."

Mrs. Latham put her hand on the top of my head and walked with me toward the cafeteria. She said, "Every day."

In the Bleak Midwinter

by Bailey White

A great fan," said Jim Wade, "sixteen-inch, sidewinder os-cillator." He slid the lever to High, and the fan wearily lumbered into action. It took a while, but by the time it got going, Christmas cards were flying across the room, and Ethel could feel tears blowing out of the corners of her eyes. "Now what do you think," Jim Wade said, "is that the world's greatest fan, or what?"

It was a 1919 General Electric, three speeds, with copper blades that showed up as a golden glow at the root of the gale. One of the blades had a jagged chipped edge that threw the fan a little off bal-ance and set up a vibration that caused the whole store to rattle and shake. A pair of Mr. and Mrs. Santa salt and pepper shakers marched with wobbly steps to the edge of their shelf. Ethel caught Mrs. Santa (salt) just as she began to tip.

"Let her go," said Jim Wade. "Tacky consignment junk. Let her hit that concrete floor and smash into a thousand pieces. People bring this stuff in here, expect me to sell it. And you know the sad-dest thing, Ethel? I do sell it." He slid the switch to Medium, then Low, and stood by the fan with his eyes closed.

"I can see this fan in your house, Ethel, on Low, a summer

night. I see a tomato sandwich, a jar of capers; the doors are open to the evening breeze, nothing but the sound of crickets."

But it was December, Ethel was looking for a woodstove, not an electric fan, and in the background chipmunks were singing "Silent Night."

"Jim Wade," said Ethel, sliding the switch back to Off, "it was fifteen degrees last night. No one wants to hear about the evening breeze."

"It's a habit of mine," said Jim Wade wistfully, "daydreaming in other seasons. Do you daydream in other seasons, Ethel?" But in a far corner of the store Ethel had found a beautiful woodstove, with a nickel-plated fender and a gleaming finial.

"On no!" Jim Wade said, swooping in on her, "Oh no!" He stood in front of the stove and held Ethel off with one hand. "A great old stove from the 1890s, you're thinking to yourself? Maybe Birmingham Iron Works, you're thinking to yourself? You *think*." He paused dramatically. "Made in Taiwan, early eighties—NINETEEN eighties. See this? Phillips head screws. Junk! An imitation of nothing that ever existed, designed by tricksters to bring back memories that nobody ever had. Three hundred and fifty dollars, a ridiculous price for a fake stove. And you know what, Ethel? Some woman will come in here wearing a green dirndl skirt and a shirt with red piping on the collar and buy the thing! She'll put an arrangement of artificial flowers on the lid. Flowers on top of a woodstove, Ethel, just think about it! Country charm!"

"Oh, Jim Wade," said Ethel. "'Tis the season to be jolly."

"Ethel," said Jim Wade, "one thing and one thing only would make me jolly."

"Don't start, Jim Wade," said Ethel. "Help me find a woodstove. I want to heat my house with boat scraps."

"The stove you want isn't here," said Jim Wade, and he flipped the sign on the Antique Mall to CLOSED and locked the door. "The stove you want is a Columbus Stove and Range model—a Little Bungalow—out at Paramore Surplus."

Jim Wade turned on the heat in his van and they roared through town, past the Christmas tree on the courthouse lawn, past the Salvation Army woman in her short red skirt prancing up and down in the cold on the corner of Jackson and Broad, past the ten-thousand-dollar display of lights at Flowers Industries, and out onto Highway 84.

"Marry me, Ethel!" cried Jim Wade, turning loose of the steering wheel and slapping the dashboard with both hands. "This spring, in Saint Louis, the fan manufacturing capital of the U.S., marry me!"

"You missed it," said Ethel. "You should have turned on one-eleven."

"GOT A NICE FAN out back," said Mrs. Paramore, glaring up at Jim Wade. "Old Emerson model." Her stringy, blue-veined feet, in silver lamé slippers, were propped up on a little gas space heater, and a pair of Santa Claus earrings swung violently from her weary earlobes. Ethel found the woodstove under a pile of tin bathtubs half full of rusty ice water and frozen mosquito wigglers, and bloodied her knuckles untangling it from a pile of copper and iron weather vanes—roosters and trotting horses and a cow and a pig pointing north, south, east, and west.

"Twenty-five for the stove, fifty-five dollars for the fan, firm," said Mrs. Paramore, clamping her thin lips onto her cigarette and crossing her arms over the skinny blue iron-on Victorian Santa Claus on her sweatshirt. "That's an Emerson."

"But look at this oil cup!" wailed Jim Wade. "Look at this cheap motor! This is not the fine hollow-core Emerson motor of the twenties and thirties! This is a wartime Emerson!"

Ethel left her money on the counter, and in the parking lot she made a ramp out of two two-by-sixes and heaved and shoved the stove into the back of Jim Wade's van.

"Look at this wrinkle finish!" Jim Wade's voice rang out across the grim fields of scrap metal, car parts, and pieces of houses. "Look at this cross guard!"

"It's an Emerson fan. My prices is firm," smacked Mrs. Paramore. The Santa Claus earrings snatched and bobbed emphatically, stretching the holes in her earlobes to vicious little slits. "I don't dicker."

"I swear, Ethel," said Jim Wade, roaring back down Highway 84, "I should be under the care of a psychoanalyst, or at the very least I should be spending six hours a day under a two-hundred-watt bulb reading the short stories of Somerset Maugham."

"Seasonal affect disorder, that's what they call it," said Ethel, nursing her scraped knuckles.

"Instead I'm eking my life away down in that store," said Jim Wade, "selling male-end-only strings of Christmas lights to overweight women dressed in clothes that blink. I'm a danger to myself and others, Ethel. So watch out."

At Ethel's house they struggled with the stove up the stairs to the strains of "Joy to the World" wafting across the park from the loudspeakers downtown. Ethel began snapping sections of stovepipe together while Jim Wade unscrewed the oil cup on her little Emerson Seabreeze.

"Who but you, Ethel, would know to use Royal Purple?" he sighed. "Look at this"— and he spread his arms and made a slow spin. The elegant little sailboat hung in a sling from the ceiling, and one corner of the room was filled with wood scraps in neat stacks, but the Portsmouth boatbuilder had taken his tools back to New Hampshire early in the fall and Ethel had swept up the shavings and sawdust and put the furniture back. "No garlands of greenery, no stockings hung by the chimney with care, no bandsawed plywood reindeer prancing across the wall," said Jim Wade, "just the simple, functional home of a capable woman who knows how to take care of an Emerson desk fan."

"Get your side," said Ethel, snapping in the last section of pipe, and together they lifted the stove up and settled it into place. Ethel jammed the elbow into the ceramic thimble and stood back.

"Wooo!" she said, crumpling up newspapers and stuffing scraps of poplar and pine into the little front door of the stove. "Give me a match, Jim Wade, turn off that fan!"

Behind the little isinglass window of the stove door the flames flickered and danced. It was cold outside, another freezing night. Ethel had brought her plants in, and the warmth from the stove spread the rich loamy smell all through the room. Jim Wade started water boiling for tea while Ethel checked the tightness of the stovepipe joints with gloved hands.

"I will never understand the mystique of boats," said Jim Wade. "All that business about the lonely sea and the sky and a star to steer her by. To me it just seems damp and cold, with an enormous potential for danger. Was that it, Ethel, that heady feeling that is said to come over us right before a violent death? Because I never could figure it out, to me he just seemed like a bandy-legged little man with a funny-looking saw, he never said anything, and he always smelled like glue every time I saw him. What I want to know, Ethel, is, why did it have to be boats in particular, instead of, say, electric desk fans?"

"It doesn't have anything to do with boats or fans, Jim Wade," said Ethel. "Stop trying to figure it out."

The wood scraps were very dry, and the fire had gotten so hot that the stove had begun making rhythmic sucking gulps: *whomp whomp whomp.*

"Here we are, two lonely people huddled around a pitiful spark," Jim Wade said. "'Earth as hard as iron, water like a stone.'"

"I am not lonely, Jim Wade," said Ethel, closing the vent down hard and snapping the damper shut. "And this is not a pitiful spark. We may see flashover any second now."

"'In the bleak midwinter,'" said Jim Wade.

"The bleak midwinter has its benefits," said Ethel. "Just think of the fleas that might have tormented dogs and cats next July, now being killed by this cold snap."

The roaring in the stove settled down to a low rustling murmur. Ethel and Jim Wade sat drinking their tea and listening to the little clicks and taps and rumbles as the stove adjusted to its heat and the firewood slumped into the ashes.

Then, inspired perhaps by the gleaming blades of the well-oiled Emerson Seabreeze, or the summery smells of green plants, or the flickering glow through the little window in the door of the stove — the last remnants of the Portsmouth boatwright going up in smoke — Jim Wade leaned over and gave Ethel a kiss. But it was an ill-placed kiss that landed on the angle of her jaw, and Jim Wade was left with the impression of a hard, sharp edge against his lips.

His van didn't have time to warm up on the short drive to his house, and he sat at the stoplight, feeling the cold wrap around his legs, and tried to imagine himself heading west on 84, away from all the glitter and sparkle of Christmas, through the narrow winter days, and right out the other side to summertime in some vast Midwestern state where the blades of electric fans would spin and the air would be filled with the hum of their hollow-shaft motors — Zephair, Northwind, Seabreeze, Vortalex, Star Rite. But it was cold and dark — the bleak midwinter — and as he drove past the tiny white lights twinkling so cheerily on the azalea bushes in the park, he found that he couldn't think about anything but the deaths of fleas.

A Southern Christmas

by Ellen Gilchrist

I had meant to tell you about Southern Christmases. I thought I would begin by saying the men spent the morning with their wives and the afternoon with their mistresses. But that was later, after we were corrupted by prosperity. Instead, I decided to tell about a Christmas that was long ago, in a time of innocence and war.

Christmases everywhere and in all times are fraught with danger and with sadness. It is the winter equinox. The festivals of all cultures at this time of year are meant to bring light to the darkness of winter. This is what the Jesus story is all about. The birth of hope. If winter comes, can spring be far behind? Or, as the poet Wallace Stevens wrote, "One must have a mind of winter to regard the frost and the boughs of the pine-trees crusted with snow . . . and not to think of any misery in the sound of the wind. . . ."

I have always had a mind of winter. I have always looked askance at the efforts people make to cheer themselves up. I think this is because I loved the preparations for Christmas so much, when I was a child, that the letdown when it was over was more than I could bear. Later, when I was part of a theater group, the same thing would happen to me at the end of the play. We would be producing *Tiny Alice*, by Edward Albee, let us say. We would build a fabulous set, rehearse the play forty times, perform it ten times, then it would all be over. The curtain would fall, the audience would go home, we would read the reviews, fini.

The Christmases I most vividly remember took place during the Second World War, when my Southern family was living in small towns in the Midwest. My father was an engineer, in charge of building airfields for the Army Air Corps. There was not much stuff in the United States during the Second World War. Most of the rubber and sugar and steel and gasoline and manufactured goods were being used to fight Germany and Japan. Everyone was a conservationist and a recycler. No one would have thought of wasting anything or complaining because there was no sugar. The only new household goods that we acquired for several years were black blinds to pull down during air-raid drills. I was very proud of those blinds and was reasonably sure they would keep my night light from guiding German bombers to Seymour, Indiana, but not certain that they would. I would have felt better if we could have taped them down with adhesive tape.

It was in this atmosphere that my eighth Christmas came. For many weeks secrets were being kept in every corner of our small stucco house. My mother's beautiful cousin Nell, whose husband had been killed in the war, was staying with us. Across the street our neighbors' house had a gold star in the window and a black wreath on the door. Their son had died somewhere in Europe. Our next-door neighbors had two sons in the Navy. My brothers and I were the only children on the block.

I was making my older brother, Dooley, a book that had the schedules of all the nightly radio programs glued to the pages along with some cartoons from the Sunday funny papers and a patriotic poem I had written. I was gluing the things to the pages with glue made from flour and water. While it worked well as an adhesive, it sometimes obscured part of the writing. I wasn't worried. Dooley and I knew the radio schedules by heart anyway. I knew that at six o'clock on Monday night *Inner Sanctum* would come on, and I could either go on and listen to it and have bad dreams all night, or not listen to it and have dreams about a terrible story I imagined it telling. The theme of the stories was usually along the lines of "murder will out."

So I was working on my present for Dooley and spending Saturday afternoons shopping at the five-and-ten-cent stores trying to decide what to buy my mother and my baby brother with the small amount of money I had saved from my allowance. I finally bought my mother a tiny little terra-cotta planter made in Mexico. She still has it and keeps it proudly on a shelf beside her leather-bound editions of Shakespeare and Cervantes and Milton.

Dooley was keeping his door locked and giving me knowing looks. He knew it drove me crazy to keep secrets or have secrets kept from me. He knew that by the 22nd of December I would start trying to cut deals with him, offering to tell him what I had for him in exchange for information about what I was going to get.

I was pretty sure I didn't believe in Santa Claus, but my parents were so adamant in their belief that I always began to waver as the time drew near.

The spirit of Christmas was so rich and strong that year, even I was subject to its powers. And with good cause. In the weeks preceding Christmas Eve my mother and my cousin and the women in our neighborhood were preparing a surprise for me that I would remember all my life. In the dark of winter, the darkest months of the Second World War, in the face of their mourning, these women were spending hours every night making me a doll's wardrobe the likes of which I have never seen since. A wealthy contractor my parents had for dinner one night had sent my father a fabulous doll for me. He had thought I was cute, I suppose, or else he was just as sad and burdened that winter as the rest of the United States. I remember his face the night he ate with us, and the sadness in his hands and eyes as he talked to me. Perhaps I had shown him the book I was making Dooley. Perhaps he liked little messy redheaded girls who never combed their hair and slept with a night light to make up for listening to *Inner Sanctum*.

Anyway, he had mailed this fabulous doll to my parents to give to me, and my mother and her friends had decided to make a wardrobe for the doll. Out of old clothes they had fashioned a complete wardrobe. There was a light blue coat trimmed with real leopard fur. There was a leopard hat. There was a nightgown with lace and a matching robe. There were knitted slippers and a dark red jersey dress for afternoons. There were aprons and a sunsuit. There were cotton underpants and several petticoats.

The doll had come dressed in a black and white checked taffeta evening dress and silk stockings and evening shoes. She had black hair and black eyes and little breasts and a lovely smile.

The other present I received was a toy washing machine with a wringer. It was an exact model of the one my mother had hooked up in the basement of the stucco house. When she used the machine it was my job to stand by with a broom to knock her down in case she got electrocuted.

At our house the children's presents from Santa Claus were never wrapped up. They were left beneath our stockings during the night and as soon as we woke on Christmas morning we would run into the living room to see "what we got." My family was much too excitable to have a routine that was any more structured than that.

I slept in my room part of the night. Then I slept in between my parents for a while. Then I slept at the foot of Dooley's bed, a boon that cost me five cents or ten poker chips on ordinary nights. Sometime during that night I may actually have been asleep for a while. As I said, the spirit of Christmas was very powerful that year.

At dawn I ran down the stairs with Dooley right behind me. And there was the doll. She sat on my mother's slipcovered sofa in all her fabulous beauty. Her wonderful clothes were lying all around her. It was a present for a king's child. I could not even touch it. I could not even scream. Off to the side was the washing machine.

Dooley was running his hand up and down the barrel of a BB gun and watching me happily. He had known all along. Only eleven years old and he had been able to keep a secret of this magnitude.

My mother appeared with my father and my cousin behind her. I sat down on the floor and began to undress my doll. Off came the evening dress and the stockings and the shoes. On went the underpants, the jersey dress, the coat and hat. Off came the underpants and coat and hat and dress, on went the nightgown and the robe. This went on for half an hour while Dooley cocked and uncocked the BB gun and the baby woke up and was brought into the room and given his toys and my father read the Christmas cards from our distant relatives out loud. My mother went into the kitchen and made scrambled eggs and cinnamon toast with lots of rationed sugar. At ten o'clock I put my doll into a stroller and went to pay calls on the neighbors who had helped make the wardrobe. I strolled my doll from house to house. I went inside and had conversations and ate cookies and examined Christmas trees.

The day wore on into afternoon. My mother and father and the baby went to sleep for a nap. I played with my doll awhile, then I had an idea. I took the toy washing machine down to the basement and set it up beside my mother's. I filled it with soap and water. I took the new doll clothes and began to stuff them in the washing machine. I was almost finished and was just stuffing in the blue wool coat with the leopard collar when my mother came down the stairs and found me. She began to cry. I had never seen my mother cry except at death, but now she cried like a child. She didn't get mad. She didn't yell. She just sat on the stairs and cried. I remember being surprised by all of this. I was completely happy, sitting on the floor with my washing machine full of soapy water. The clothes still looked all right to me. Especially the lace-trimmed robe with rainbows of soap bubbles in the lace.

If my mother had been older or more cynical, she might have said to herself, a typical Christmas afternoon. At least someone didn't get shot in a hunting accident or get drunk and fall down the stairs. As it was, she used the afternoon the way humans often do. She turned it into a story. By January and February and March, as spring came and the tide of war turned in Germany, the women in the neighborhood began to tell the story. Over their bridge tables and when they met on the sidewalk in the afternoon, they would tell it and dissolve in laughter. The more they told it, the funnier it became. It's still a pretty good Christmas story.

The Road to Tarshish

by Aaron Gwyn

*"And should I not pity Nineveh, that great city,
in which are more than one hundred and twenty
thousand persons who cannot discern between their
right hand and their left?" Jonah 4:11*

It was winter, while attending prayer meeting with his parents, that Leroy Crider received the call to preach. For half an hour, the boy had been kneeling at a couch between his uncle and father, ignored as children are, and when his eyes grew wet and his lips began to stammer, he lost track of his surroundings. The next thing he would remember was his father lifting him in his arms and holding him toward the ceiling, announcing to the room that his son had been called by God Almighty to be witness to the lost.

Confident of the calling, Leroy never worried when he would begin his ministry. He was short, thickset and sturdy, grew up rambunctious, fancying himself invulnerable in a fight. He worked odd jobs throughout his teens, and after he returned from the war in Europe, he married a woman from Texas and began working in the oilfield. His commitment to his proper vocation was strong as ever, but at the time he was making exceptional wages, and the money, Leroy decided, would be a great help when he and his wife began evangelizing.

By the age of fifty-two, he was foreman of a drilling rig off the coast of southern California, six months away from retirement. His sister Oma had recently purchased three hundred sixty acres outside Perser, Oklahoma, and when she promised him a parcel of the acreage, she told him it was an offering; she had been anxious for him to begin preaching since she was a child.

So in the fall of 1971, Leroy moved his wife and himself to Oklahoma, purchased a double-wide trailer and had it set on the east side of his sister's pond, right amongst a scattered stand of oaks. They spent the first several years getting their lands in order, Leroy particular about the grounds, Louise about the house's decoration and cleaning. When they were well settled, Leroy took the pastorship of a rural Pentecostal church but soon resigned out of disgust. The church, he would often explain, was lifeless, and it would have taken Christ himself to rouse the congregation. He would still preach special engagements when asked but eventually dropped the pretense of being a minister entirely. Other things, he would tell his sister, needed his attention, and at the time, his grandson had come to live with him.

One day when he was washing the '63 Mercury he'd recently restored, Leroy felt a pain in his chest. After a few moments his breath grew short, the pain worse. He walked inside the house, into the kitchen where Louise was washing dishes. She took a look at him and flipped off the tap.

"What's wrong?" she asked.

Leroy did not answer. He began to rifle the cabinet.

"Daddy," she said, "what's the matter?"

"Enchiladas," he told her, and finding the roll of antacids, tore away the paper and popped several in his mouth. But as the afternoon wore on, the stinging under his breastbone grew worse, and sitting in his recliner, Leroy called his wife in from the kitchen. "Mama," he said, wincing, "better phone next door. Call and see if Pete will run me down to emergency."

Louise walked over and picked up the receiver. It had been thirty years since she'd driven further than her mailbox.

THE DOCTORS SAID Leroy had had a mild heart attack, and when they sent him to Oklahoma City for tests, found a blockage. They quickly admitted him to the hospital, performing a bypass two days later. Leroy came through the surgery with an encouraging prognosis. His specialist was pleased with how the procedure had gone and allowed him to return home in under a week.

Though they told him a man in his health would see a prompt recovery, Leroy did not find it so. Walking from one end of his house to the other would exhaust him, and his son-in-law had to install a seat in the shower. The old man would sit there, Louise on the other side of the curtain, steam fogging the windows and mirrors. "Dad," she would ask him, "are you alright?" and several moments would pass before his baritone reverberated the walls in answer.

Louise knew that many men of his generation would have had difficulty accepting such a reduction of their strength, but her husband was not one of these. Back when he and his sister had done nursing home visitation, she'd remarked on a woman she saw being cleaned by two interns.

"Lord," Oma whispered, "I hope that never happens to me."

Leroy looked at her, shook his head. "We live long enough," he told Oma, "they'll be wiping my hind end and yours both."

But while he did not struggle against his weakness, social interaction began to make him increasingly nervous. He'd always been one to hold the center of attention. He liked to tell stories of his younger days. For hours he'd sit telling how, after he'd run a small chainsaw through his hand, he bonded the skin with Super Glue. He'd tell about refusing to use a jack when he changed the tires on his car, picking up the front end and kicking blocks beneath its axles; how, in the town of Blisten, Utah, he'd once saved a woman from being raped. His audience enjoyed listening to these tales, even though they knew the particulars by heart, that their teller would assume the role of hero in each. But now Leroy found noise of any kind, be it conversation, radio, television, or traffic, put him on edge. He much preferred being alone.

He began spending his days in the sunroom he'd built a few years prior. The room had an air conditioner and gas heater, and its wood-paneled walls were hung with farm implements and pictures of rigs he'd worked on, platform and deep-sea. Two of the walls were comprised entirely of windows, and from his recliner Leroy could look out over the large pond that stood between his and Oma's land.

The pond was old and anglers from around the country had pulled catfish from it long as a man's arm. Woods bordered it on either end, cattails sprouted from its shallower side, and the old man's lawn sloped toward its shore in a long, unbroken sward. While many of the ponds in the Midwest were murky, this one was well settled, the surface very clear. In the spring the water carried a slight green tint, in the fall, a brown. During the winter the entire pond would freeze down to three feet. Leroy's brother-in-law would walk to its center, chisel out disks of ice with a posthole digger, and set a stool near its edge to fish.

As the days wore on, Leroy began to find that the pond reassured him. Like a child at a movie, he would sit on the edge of his chair watching turtles and snakes cross from one bank to another, beavers, muskrats, and water moccasins. In the early morning crappie would surface to feed; in the evening, bass. He kept a notebook beside him so he could chart their habits, passing these to his daughter who lived up the road and enjoyed walking down in the cool of the day to fish.

Having been explained Leroy's regimen, the doctors said it was perfect for his recovery, that a combination of time and rest would return him to much his prior state. He'd sit in his recliner thinking of this — sturdy old man with silver hair bushing the sides of his head, a round face not so much wrinkled as creased—watching the sun decline below the black oaks at the pond's farther side, casting the surface of the water in shadow.

It was along this time, along the time his incision began to turn from bright red to pink, that Leroy awoke from a long nap and noticed the figure of a man walking the bank on the pond's far side. He thought nothing of it. His sister often let neighbors come in to fish, and sometimes his nephew would have people over to roast hot dogs on a spit of sand which jutted from the shore.

But when he phoned Oma later that week, his news upset her. "What'd he look like," she asked. "Was he blond?"

"Oma," he said, "I don't know. He was too far away."

"We haven't had anybody down there fishing for a month."

"Well."

"Was he tall?"

"I told you I could just make him out. Couldn't tell you it was even a 'him.'"

The phone grew quiet for a few moments, and Oma asked would he give a call if the man returned. "Just call over," she told him, "don't try to say anything to him yourself. Pete will be chomping at the bit to get down there and wave that gun of his around."

Leroy began keeping a vigil, thinking of it more as something to occupy his mind than a precaution. All through the summer afternoons he'd sit in his recliner with coveralls unzipped to his sternum, peering through a pair of service binoculars on occasion, drawing a hand to his chest to finger the scar.

The season went by without further incident. His daughter and son-in-law purchased a house in town; his grandson called to tell them about Oregon; Bobby Hassler, his former pastor, stopped to see when he might return to church. Then one day when his daughter had driven his wife to Tulsa, Leroy returned from the bathroom and saw the slender form standing down on the pond bank, this time a hundred yards closer. Leroy fetched up his binoculars, fitted them to his eyes, but already the man had begun his ascent into the orange-tipped leaves.

He sat for a long while scanning the autumn tree line, then dropped his hands into his lap. Before the man had vanished, Leroy was certain the lenses had shown him a naked and filthy haunch, pulled without hurry behind the trunk of a large elm.

"You're sure?" Oma asked.

"I'm positive," Leroy told her. "He was down there without a stitch of clothes on him."

They were at his sister's house later that evening, Leroy, his wife, Oma, and her husband, sitting around the dinner table drinking decaffeinated coffee.

Leroy pointed toward an east window from which the pond could be seen. "Had to've been close as that bird feeder."

"Did you see what he looked like?" his brother-in-law asked.

Leroy shook his head. "I didn't."

Pete tightened his mouth, raised his head a bit, and glancing out the window, watched a squirrel run the length of a blackjack.

"It could be a mental patient," Oma offered.

"A who?" her husband asked.

"You're always hearing about some mental patient getting away." Oma began to laugh nervously. "Maybe he's down there living in the woods."

The three stared at her.

"I'm the one who's here by myself all day," she protested. "Probably end up getting raped and robbed."

"Oma," Louise said, "you will not."

Oma leaned out and touched Louise on the arm. "My luck, just robbed."

"Oma!" her sister-in-law chastened.

"Well," she said.

The couples sat longer discussing the situation, who the man might be, what they might tell the sheriff's office if they decided to report the incident. Oma rose to make more coffee, and soon the conversation switched to Leroy's health, and after another half hour, whether he might be able to preach one day.

"Tell you the truth," he said, his face reddening slightly, "I haven't given it much thought."

Louise put her hand over her husband's. "Right now," she said, "we're just getting him back where he needs to be."

"You'll get there," Pete told him.

They chatted for a while longer, Pete and Louise carrying the conversation. Finally Oma shook her head and interrupted them. "I wasn't trying to pressure anybody," she said.

"Not the way it sounded to me," said Leroy.

"I was only—"

"You want somebody to preach so bad, why don't you do it?"

Oma sipped her coffee a moment. "Don't be hateful," she said.

They continued this way, their voices growing louder. After a few minutes, Pete picked up his cup by the handle, pushed his chair back, and stood. "Y'all," he told them, "I'm going to bed."

"You working in the morning?" asked Louise.

"Yes ma'am."

"Good night," said Leroy.

Pete patted Leroy's shoulder and left the room, leaving his wife and in-laws in silence.

The family was used to such exchanges. Before Leroy's heart attack, the disputes would get severe and terminate in the brother and sister's not speaking to each other for weeks. Oma's position was that a couple with as little obligation as her brother and his wife were squandering their vocation by refusing to evangelize, that such people under the divine anointing could keep many from the fires of hell. Leroy's position was that it was none of his sister's business, and if he'd known she'd hold the land over his head, he would never have moved on to it.

They sat longer, and soon Louise made an excuse for her and her husband to leave. Oma walked them out to their car, stood at the garage door in her bare feet.

"You call over here you see any more naked men," Oma joked, trying to coax a smile from her brother.

"We will," Louise told her.

Leroy slid into the car without comment.

ALTHOUGH THE QUARREL had angered him, Leroy continued his watch. Twice more he saw the man, and after he'd called next door to inform his relatives, a deputy drove out one morning and walked the pond's perimeter. Leroy stood on the shore with his sister and wife, watching his brother-in-law and the deputy beat paths through the grass, stopping on occasion to examine patches of ground. It took them half an hour to make the circuit, and when they returned to where Leroy was standing, they had little to report.

"Couldn't see any tracks," the deputy told him, removing his hat and wiping at his forehead. "But that don't mean anything, dry as it's been."

Leroy nodded, looked briefly to the ground.

"You say he was naked?" the deputy asked.

"Was when I saw him," said Leroy.

"Can you give any more in the way of description?"

"He was a tall fellow," Leroy told him. "About six foot."

"White?" asked the deputy, writing.

"Mm-hmm."

"Color hair?"

"Bald," answered Leroy.

"Did you get a look at his face?"

"I didn't."

The deputy continued writing for a moment, then flipped the notebook shut and replaced it in his pocket.

"Well," he said, "give a ring if he comes back around. Other than that . . ." The man trailed off and gave his pen a click.

"Can you send someone by now and then?" Leroy asked. "Maybe just—"

The deputy shook his head. "We just don't have the men."

"I'd feel safer if you could," Oma told him.

"Y'all have guns?" the deputy asked.

Both Pete and Leroy said they did.

"Man like that came into my yard—" the deputy stopped, scraped his teeth across his bottom lip.

"Can we do that?" Louise asked.

"Long as you drag him in the house afterwards and say he was breaking in."

His listeners stared at him.

"You didn't hear it from me, though." The deputy turned toward the driveway and the four escorted him up the hill.

"Do you have any idea who it could be?" Oma asked as they neared his car.

"Couldn't say, Mrs. Thacker. They just opened a mental hospital over in Okemah. Might call and see if they're missing anybody."

Oma elbowed Leroy in the ribs, shot him a look her brother did not return.

ANOTHER WEEK WENT by and the man did not show himself. Leroy continued watching, but after the fourth day of seeing nothing his attention began to flag. Recently his health had begun improving, and he was getting out in the yard to do light work. Over the past months he'd found it torturous to watch the boy from up the street push a mower around his lawn without consideration for shape or symmetry.

The day Leroy started his riding mower felt to him like a revival. He drove it as if on parade, steering the machine around the plum and apple trees, flower beds and stone steps. He did not trim closely. He set the blade high so the day after he might perform the task again. Louise watched from the window with a look of concern, and when her husband finished the job, took him a glass of water and complimented his work.

Little by little, Leroy fell into his old habits. As his strength came back, so did his desire for fellowship, and he and Louise began to socialize. He would have a week of days where he felt much the same as ever, others where he would be tired and only want to lie on the couch. But these seemed fewer as time went by, and he had every hope of returning to his former health.

Along this time a series of thunderstorms hit Oklahoma and for days dumped inches of rain on the buildings and farmlands of Perser County. Leroy sat by the window, watching rain fall and water climb the pond bank. Just when the sun would come out and the grass would seem to have dried, more clouds would gather in the west, dark billows piled at the horizon's edge.

When the rains finally ceased and several days of sun dried his lawn, Leroy went out just after sunrise and started his mower, thinking that this would be his last opportunity to cut grass before the fast-approaching winter—there were already brown patches that would not come green again till spring. He blazed a swath alongside his driveway, and as he doubled back to the house, he saw Louise at the window sipping her morning coffee. He raised his hand and she returned the gesture by smiling, shaking toward him a finger of warning.

Leroy cut grass most of the morning, his mower bogging in places, having to be unstuck. He would slide the machine into neutral, get in back of it and push, all the while glancing toward the house where Louise watched him, shaking her head. He pretended not to see her, attempting to conceal how winded the task made him as he walked back to the mower and climbed astraddle. The third time he freed the contraption, pushing it out of a sinkhole, specks swam before his eyes, and he very nearly collapsed.

It was close to lunchtime, and Leroy was making a final pass across the backyard, just rounding the front corner of the house, when he glanced behind him and saw the tall, thin man leaning naked against the fence. His mouth was mumbling, and Leroy was struck with the thought that only the sound of the lawn mower drowned a string of profanities. He flipped the emergency shutoff and darted inside. Flinging open the door to the hall closet, he fetched his twelve gauge, shucked a shell into its chamber, and was soon moving across the living room, his wife hurling questions at his heels.

He went out the back, shuffled quickly down the steps, making for the rear gate. He did not reach it. Halfway across the lawn he stopped and let the barrel of the weapon fall against his shin. He stood there looking up the fence line to the north, back down it to the south.

Louise was soon beside him, tapping his shoulder. "Daddy," she was saying, "what is it?"

Leroy started moving again, and she followed him along the fence. He crouched, stood the rifle on its butt, and searched the ground as if looking for change. After a while he rose, studied his wife's face for a moment, and turned to walk away.

"What is it?" Louise called after him.

"Cottonmouth," he said.

Leroy was certain of the place where the man had stood — a patch of mud three fence posts from the gate — but there was not a footprint near it other than his own.

Later in the afternoon, when Louise was napping, he slid a pistol in his hip pocket and walked back along the fence, studying the ground's every crevice. He went at the task for half an hour and then walked slowly toward the house.

THAT NIGHT HE LAY beside his wife, staring at the rotating blades of the ceiling fan. From the pond the season's final frogs croaked loudly to each other, and hearing them, Leroy could not sleep.

He pulled the sheet to his hips and looked at Louise, her face shaded and strange in the half-light. Though the windows were shut, the air-conditioning running, Leroy thought he could smell wood and leaf from outside, the late autumn damp. These were scents he remembered from his childhood in the Quachita forest, lying awake in his room listening to the elders visiting late into the night. On occasion they would talk about visions that the Lord had given them: visions of heaven, and hell, and those departed. Sometimes he would creep up the hallway and kneel beside the kitchen table to better hear their conversations. As they understood it, the world of the spirit commingled with the world of the flesh, and within the overlap, revelation was imminent. Further, they held there were some whom God had chosen to be the receivers of these messages, some more attuned to the workings of the spirit.

As the years went by, Leroy thought this might well be the case. Out of a family of nine children, all but two—he and his brother Freddie, who'd died at the age of eight—had witnessed a visual manifestation of that other world layered atop their own. His brother, after falling from an oil derrick, had beheld a cloud of demons coming to take him; his sisters, crashing their station wagon into the side of an overpass, had seen angels of the Lord standing as protectors. His mother would often tell how she had fist fought the Devil when he came to her in the form of an up-reared lion. Leroy thought that perhaps his time for visions had arrived as well.

He lay thinking of this, troubled by the fact that the meaning of his family's visions was immediately apparent. They were a call to repentance, or a message of assurance, or a symbol of victory. But, running through a list of portents and omens, he could not think what a naked trespasser was apropos of. Perhaps, he thought, it meant nothing, and his sister was right about the man being a mental patient.

The next night he again lay sleepless, thinking of Oma's conclusion, and the more he thought of it, the more it angered him. Though he cared for her, he did not want to believe she could have an opinion about such things. She was the youngest member of the family, and he'd always played the role of the older brother with success and influence. He didn't want to hear her opinions, whether they concerned a trespasser he had seen or a calling he should answer.

He lay longer, became angrier yet. His sister thought she knew the answer to every puzzle; she thought she knew how others should live their lives. During the three months he'd been pastor of his church, she sat on the front row beaming approval, but Leroy decided if she'd once looked out over the congregation, looked out over faces that showed no signs of interest or adoration, she'd never have said a word to him when he resigned. Give him the chance to tell a story about his boyhood, or the oil field, or an exercise of strength, and Leroy could have mesmerized any audience in the States. Hand him a Bible and ask him to deliver a sermon, and his listeners' eyes would glaze.

His sister did not understand this, and it surprised him that she hadn't tried to link the trespasser with his calling in some way, saying that he was a judgment upon him. It would, Leroy decided, be just like her.

Then the next night came, and still Leroy could not sleep, could not shake Oma from his mind. A week went past. A cold month followed. Night after night, as the grass bleached and the sky whitened and his wife decorated their home with candy canes and stencil, something rose in him like a vapor through dense air, and an interpretation of his vision — if vision it was — presented itself. Starting from somewhere in his recesses and moving forward in a cloud, the understanding began to sharpen, coming clearer and clearer until it sat behind his brow like a revolving gear. He had been given the call to bring souls to Christ and had patly refused. What if, Leroy began to wonder, those souls had not found another witness? What if he alone had been responsible for their salvation?

He turned on his side, pulled the cool edge of the pillow against his cheek, and shook the thought from himself. This was not, he decided, the way the Lord worked. Lost souls did not arise from the grave to trouble those who might have brought them succor. It ran counter to the Word of God, was not scriptural. Under his breath he whispered the words of Apostle Paul on the matter: "It is appointed unto man once to die, and after that the judgment."

But, although Leroy had found biblical support, the thought continued returning, and at night he lay with the notion grinding in his head, the suspicion that the man was a vision, a spirit broken free of its realm. This circled his mind, over and over, could not be put away. And sometime, right before dawn, Leroy got out of bed, slipped into his robe, and went down the hallway to the living room.

After glancing anxiously out the window, he stoked the fireplace and sank onto the couch, flipping on a light, retrieving his Bible from the coffee table in front of him. He thumbed through it a while, until he found the passage he sought. He sat there, reading glasses pushed down his nose, scanning the verse his sister had marked for him, underlined in red ink:

When I say unto the wicked: O wicked man, thou shalt surely die, and thou dost not speak to this man, to warn the wicked from his way; that wicked man shall die in his iniquity; but his blood will I require at thy hands.

IT WAS IN THE DIM time of evening, two days before Christmas, when, bleary eyed and short on sleep, Leroy straightened from shoveling the back deck and saw the naked man standing just inside his yard, straddling the snow covered rut where his lawn mower had bogged a few months prior. Startled, he moved away, shuffling backward a few steps. He wiped the cold from his eyes and studied the intruder, feeling the blood pounding his temples.

The man was much taller than he'd thought, close on six and a half feet, and the flesh where it stretched tight across his ribs made him look taller yet. He was filthy, his finger- and toenails blackened. His face was long and sharp angled, his chin strongly cleft, and something behind his pale eyes seemed to burn. Leroy noticed that the man had not a single hair on him, as if a perverse and skilled barber had risen early that morning and shaved him clean.

For several minutes the two of them faced each other, Leroy's eyes jumping from the man to the pond behind him, the man staring confusedly to a place in the distance, his eyes blinking as if trying them for the first time. Leroy noted that his arms were no bigger around than zucchinis, the veins standing out, and seeing this, he broke the silence.

"I know what you are," he said, his words trailing vapor.

The man mumbled his lips, but spoke nothing. He seemed to be looking at Leroy from very far away.

"I—" Leroy's speech cracked, and he trailed off. He looked at the ground. "I can't help you," he managed.

The man stood quiet. Flying across the pond, a magpie gave its call, the noise failing as the bird moved over the water. The last edge of sun had just gone below the horizon. All around him the light was dying.

"I want to go away," Leroy said, lifting his eyes to the man. "I don't feel—"

The man stared.

"I can't do anything for you," he confessed. "I'm sick."

It was then that the man's eyes seemed to snap into focus, and for the first time, Leroy was sure the man had seen him. The man squinted, steadied himself, and began to form words, his face twisted into a scowl. His lips suggested curses, but still Leroy heard nothing, nor did steam issue from this person's mouth.

Crows called into the night. The sky spat a few flakes of snow.

"Get out of here," Leroy said, raising his voice. "Get on out of here and let me be."

The man shook his head. He didn't seem about to do that. He lifted his hand and made a gesture Leroy did not understand, continued his silent cursing.

Leroy took a step toward the house, his eyes on the dimming form in front of him, the man's angles blurring into snow-white and shadow.

"Get," he said. Again his voice cracked and he spat vapor. "Go on. Get!" Suddenly he balled his hand into a fist, took a few steps toward the man, then staggered back, retreating. The colorless face before him opened to scream; Leroy heard nothing.

"Jesus, God," he began saying, stepping slowly backward. In truth, he was calling for help, but the trembling in his voice made it sound as if he'd sworn. Turning around, he began to jog toward the house, and when he reached the steps, looked back. The man stood like an alabaster headstone, his lower jaw working in the twilight.

Leroy went up the steps, crossed the porch to the back door. As always it was locked. "Please," Leroy muttered, and had there been a witness to these parties, it would've been unclear to whom he was speaking.

Coming down off the steps, he cast about in the frozen yard, unable to choose a path that did not bring him into closer contact with the man. When he stumbled back toward the porch, he'd decided he would pound the door until he roused his wife or broke the jamb. He craned his neck and looked behind him, his breath beginning to come in spurts, his vision narrowing to a pair of distorted lenses. The darkness enfolded him like a shroud.

AFTERWARD WHEN LEROY dreamed of the incident, he would reach the top step and have forgotten where he was. At a loss, he'd run a hand across his stubble, and it would take him some time to remember he'd left his pew and was approaching the pulpit to address the congregation. Beside him stood the man, soundless and without feature, quietly nodding Leroy toward his station.

The preacher would cross the stage and look to the audience below, the naked shadows chanting their pleas, a throng of stick figures in the winter night. He'd slowly lift a hand, cast them a fatherly smile. He was their shepherd, they his flock. They sat beneath him with famished eyes, thin and frail and filled with anguish, leaning forward in anticipation of his words. And yet, as he delivered his sermon, there might be one or two near the back with their heads lowered, their faces averted from his. To these Leroy found himself preaching in exclusion of the others, until the rest of his audience had faded entirely. A bitterness began to grow inside him and he slept a fretful sleep. Many nights he'd leave the podium and walk down to seize these distracted souls by their throats, scream into their faces. But dropping his eyes to theirs, strong hands curled about their necks, he still could not determine whether or not they'd heard.

Montana Christmas

by Rick Bass

Drama! On the day of the school Christmas play, Wendy, the lead actress, is sick, throwing-up sick, fever-sick. Her part in "Santa Claus and the Wicked Wazoo" is none other than the Wazoo herself, and as an eighth grader, it's her last year to be in the play before she graduates and heads to high school down in Troy. Her classmate Karen can't take her role, because Karen is Mrs. Claus—often in the same scene as the Wicked Wazoo, whose goal is, of course, to spoil Christmas.

If Wendy doesn't rally, it will be up to our daughter Mary Katherine to learn the role—not just the forty lines, but the timing, blocking, entrances and exits, in addition to keeping her own character as Martha, a peasant girl. There are only five girls in the Yaak school this year: the eighth graders, Wendy and Karen; Mary Katherine in the fourth grade; her sister Lowry in first grade; and Chiena in kindergarten.

Mary Katherine doesn't find out about the crisis until midmorning on the day of the play but goes right to the task; she and Karen spend the day practicing, and when Mary Katherine comes home that afternoon, she's cool as a cucumber, casual and confident: not arrogant, just confident, taking pleasure in the arrival of a challenge: just another day in Paradise.

My wife, Elizabeth, and I would be jittery. I can't help but think that Mary Katherine's durable native confidence—rather than bravado—is one of the myriad benefits of her two-room log school in which all the different grades sit together and interact every day, learning lessons of responsibility and loyalty in addition to all the traditional curricula. The older students help to teach and take care of the younger ones, and I try not to ever take it for granted; it's easy to forget that it's not like this in other schools.

It's a big deal, this Christmas play. Every year the whole community shows up, hermits and all. The plays are always wonderful, and there are cookies and cakes, and after the play the kids and townspeople sing Christmas carols in the log cabin community center up near the Canadian line, in the middle of the forest, over forty miles from the nearest town of any size, and it's nothing but sweet. Some years there's a hayride afterward.

This year's play, as in all the other years, goes off perfectly. It's the strangest thing hearing Mary Katherine's deep, maniacal laugh booming from behind the curtain, preceding the villainous Wazoo's entrance. I think: Okay, if she's determined to grow up, I can still be proud of her; and it's a growing up on my part to see her come swashbuckling out from behind the curtains, still booming that laugh, determined to spoil Christmas. It's a strong feeling to see her giving to the community, the audience of adults. And I feel the same sensation when Lowry, in her pink glittering ballerina outfit, comes twirling out to center stage, hands poised over her head in a graceful, elegant ballerina pose—the Dancing Doll— and cries out, "Help, help!"

Every parent feels it, and every audience member, that this is a most excellent gift by the children to the town, but for me, with my hermit tendencies, it's also a profound realization that I don't necessarily have to pass on my less than wonderful attributes to my children. They will likely be better out in the world and already have something to give to the world, and they are giving it.

All the children are giving, breathing the breath of Christmas into all of us. Mike, an eighth grader who has killed his first deer this year, a monster whitetail buck, so we can no longer call him "Mikey," is a great Santa Claus; Karen is the calm and capable Mrs. Claus; Jed, the boisterous singing leprechaun, is the true star of the show; Kilby, Luke, Levi, and Noah are sly trolls, dressed in camouflage; Kyle's a happy elf, Lowry the Dancing Doll, Zachary the toy clown, and Chiena the troll. And that's the whole student body.

Outside it's snowing hard. The pew benches in the community center are packed shoulder to shoulder, and the woodstoves are popping. Over the course of the coming year, as during every year in small western towns, there will be disagreements among the adults, fears and accusations and misunderstandings, and sometimes plain old-fashioned chemical imbalances, but this evening, at least, the beauty and purity of the children fills the cabin with a love so dense that after the play is over we linger, not wanting it to end. When we finally open the door and step outside into the falling snow, that love is adhering to us. Some of it goes sliding off into the night woods, but a lot of it stays with us and travels home and stays for a good long while, I hope. Peace on earth and good will to men.

Such are the cycles of our lives here in this place that is still a place, this forested island that still seems to be governed partly by its own system of time rather than only by society's, that the end of one thing can feel also like the beginning of another. December is that way: the last of the deer or elk is cut and wrapped and frozen, if a hunter was fortunate enough to receive one, and the coming year's meat is stored away safely. The snow is always down to the valley floor by December—another beginning—and while the rest of the world, including our relatives in the more civilized places, enters into the full frenzy of the Christmas season, things are so much quieter up here amid a complete absence of malls. Yet in that quietness the season is no less deeply felt. It's just calm and slow, like walking in soft new snow at dusk.

The days are shorter, and with the hunting season behind us and the pressure of making meat lifted, we can sleep later. We can spend any free time skiing instead of hunting. It's the beginning of rest, of play, of being able to be more with family. We begin wrapping jars of huckleberry jam for gifts, and take the girls out into the snow for the annual Christmas card picture. Elizabeth gathers boughs of cedar and pine with which to make beautiful wreaths—

she and half a dozen other women in the valley gather to spend the days making these wreaths and then mailing them, fresh scented, to friends and family in the outside world.

The children, having warmed up on Halloween and then Thanksgiving, are fully into Christmas dreaming. Mary Katherine is dubious about Santa, while Lowry's still a true believer, though as the days progress I notice that Mary Katherine comes back across the line, if even for only one more year. It is a wonderful thing to see, made all the more poignant by the knowledge that surely this is her last year. Their Christmas lists are posted on the refrigerator. I suspect that our girls are as cutthroat and mercenary as any children anywhere—it's not like they'd be thrilled with only an orange in their stocking and, in a good year, maybe a candy cane—but I have to laugh at Lowry's list: a pencil and pencil sharpener, a Barbie (I know, I know), and, most curiously, a bottle of Wite-Out. Even Mary Katherine's list is a relief: books and CDs, a new pair of snow boots, and a pair of ski goggles.

The holiday season begins for us on the day that we go to get the Christmas tree. For as long as the girls have been able to walk, they have gone into the woods with me each year to find a tree—always a young Douglas fir, which are overabundant in many of our fire-suppressed forests and in need of thinning, literally by the millions. Yet finding the perfect one is never easy. Any tree is beautiful in the forest, but we had to bring only one home one year, proud of ourselves, to hear Elizabeth's considerably more subdued reaction and vow never again to settle for anything less than perfect. How different my life has become, in these last twenty years since I left Mississippi and my store-bought trees; and how different are my girls' lives from my own childhood in Texas, when we would sometimes whack a scraggly cedar—the bush looking like a half-plucked bird, compared to the fullness of the Montana conifers—though other years my parents would purchase a tree from a big tent set up outside a mall or in a parking lot: shoppers rather than hunters.

In this new life, this Montana life, I prepare the girls for the cutting as I would if we were going on a real hunt. On Sunday night, before they get ready for bed, I tell them that when I pick them up after school on Monday, I'll bring their cross-country skis, and that we'll go out and look for the tree. The fact that they're as thrilled with this news as if it were Christmas itself pleases me greatly, and though I know they love having regular markers of tradition and security in their lives, I know also that I love it as much as they do, and perhaps more.

It's bitterly cold when I pick them up, about fifteen degrees but with a rare breeze that makes it feel closer to zero, and the sky is its usual beautiful ragtag mix of clouds, with more snow coming any minute. I've brought a thermos of hot chocolate, and on the way home we share a cup of it, drinking it out of the screw-on cup like duck hunters, and then turn onto the little road where we always turn, and get out where we always get out.

We engage in a brief snowball fight, and then I buckle on my snowshoes, and they put on their skis, and we start up the rocky ridge, which is now covered with snow. The sky is beautiful — the color of plums, the back of a seagull, of sharks, of oyster shells — and we take turns breaking trail through the new snow like explorers. The girls remember where we are going from all the other years. They've bundled up with as many sweaters and coats as they can wear, and I have more of my own larger coats in my backpack, along with the thermos.

It pleases me to see what natural backcountry skiers they are, having grown up on skis — such a difference from my own south Texas upbringing. And those beautiful skies hanging dense above the somber blue-green mountain, and the stark winter forest through which we're skiing, also elevate my spirits. I just can't tell who is more pleased, me or the girls. As we move on through the woods, seemingly the only living creatures out and about in this vast snowscape and sleeping forest, there is a spirit that accompanies us, that emanates from the three of us — a *happiness,* to use an old and worn word — that braids together to form a larger whole. And in accompanying my daughters up the ridge, I remember dimly my own childhood thirty-five years ago.

In my experience it's rare for an adult to experience, ever again, the happiness of a child. There are a million different sorts of adult happiness, mixed in with perhaps a million different nuances — satisfaction, pride, relief, euphoria — but what I feel, moving up that hill with my daughters in the approaching winter dusk, self-sufficient, for the time being, on our skis and snowshoes, and moving deeper into the woods, is a child's simple happiness, and I cannot remember having felt that in a long, long time.

Once we reach the ridge, we begin to encounter the young firs growing in between older lodgepoles and larch, and the girls are old enough this year to be good judges of physical character, by-passing weaker or asymmetrical trees and judging also which trees are too large and which are too small. Making guesses and mental notes about certain trees that we might be able to come back and examine in years hence. But searching, still, for this year's.

We look for a long time. The wind blurs our eyes and sometimes makes far-off trees look much better than they really are; we'll ski and snowshoe down into a bowl or ravine and up the other side to some such tree, only to discover upon reaching it that it's not even remotely what we're after.

For a long time now, we have been bringing back a perfect Christmas tree, one that even Elizabeth will acknowledge is perfect, with every branch, every needle, balanced and symmetrical, a tree whose beauty exceeds any possible summation of its parts. The girls are not aware of any sort of pressure, are unable, I'm sure, to imagine anything other than success, simply because that is all they remember; I am less secure, and as the dusk deepens, we travel farther, looking hard.

We pass over the stippled, methodical trails of deer and the seemingly aimless tracks of snowshoe hares, across the tracks of a mountain lion, one which has probably not eaten in a while, because we do not hear any ravens squabbling over the remains of a kill, and so I keep the girls close to me.

We're all three beginning to grow chilled, so we duck down into a ravine and huddle beneath the shelter of a big spruce tree, as if in a little fort or clubhouse, and share another cup of hot chocolate. I bundle them further, putting my heavy overcoats over their own, and making sure their mufflers are snug; and then warmed, they're ready to play again, and climb back up out of the ravine, herringboning on their skis, only to ski right back down, again and again.

They're laughing and shrieking. I don't want to caution them to conserve their energy, to counsel moderation to their joy, though I am concerned that we're so far from the truck, with the hour so late and the evening so cold. Carefully, trying hard not to disrupt the spirit of their play, I begin to ease them back toward the truck, not following our old tracks but triangulating. They're still looking up from time to time, evaluating various trees, but in their happiness and in the fast-fading light, their critical skills seem to be diminishing, and a couple of times they urge me to take a tree that, in my opinion, is flawed: recommending one because it is "cute" and another because it is "stately."

We find the perfect tree right at dark. I spy it first and, hardly daring to believe our luck, snowshoe over to it without saying anything. I call the girls over, ask them to check it out and see what they think, wanting unanimity, and even they are excited by the beauty of the tree. After double-checking to be sure they're sure, I take my saw out of the pack, tell the tree and the forest thank you out loud like a pagan, and then saw through the sweet green bark and sap, and the tree leans over slowly, softly, lightly, and settles into the snow.

We head back to the truck, taking turns pulling the tree. It's surprisingly hard work, and the needles leave a beautiful, wandering, feathery trail behind us, completely erasing our tracks.

Unprompted, as darkness settles, the girls begin singing "Jingle Bells," and then right after that, with no prior sort of communication save that unspoken kind that exists between sisters, they break into the chant of a streetside political rally, a protest really, that we witnessed (all right, participated in) a few years ago: "What do we want? De-moc-racy! When do we want it? Now!" And in a silly singsong way, the chant seems to make perfect sense out in the middle of the unpeopled forest, in the deep cold beneath the gathering night, unseen and unheard by anyone other than our own selves.

By the time we reach the truck we're all three cold again, and after loading the tree into the back—it fills the bed and even lying on its side looks perfect—I warm up the truck, and we sit there in the cab, vapor-breathing and clouding the windshield, and drink more hot chocolate. Upon our arrival Elizabeth comes out on the porch to inspect what we have brought home to her.

She looks it over carefully.

"It's perfect," she says finally.

Long after the tree is gone, and the year, I will remember that afternoon.

Buy for Me the Rain

by Bret Anthony Johnston

On the warm January morning when Leiland Marshall buried his mother, he kept shifting in his folding chair, hoping to see Moira Jarrett. Her flight was scheduled to land before the service started, but even as the line of mourners filed by the casket, she hadn't arrived. This was in Corpus Christi, Texas, at a cemetery near the ocean, under a canvas tent that gave everything a green hue. Death had come for his mother's body in the night, had come with miserable slowness, but when women in the line asked, he said she had passed peacefully in her sleep. As he spoke he glanced over their shoulders for Moira. He watched for her as the mourners dispersed, then again when they brought sympathy and snack platters to the house. She never showed. Soon his mother's friends slipped into their dainty coats, collected purses and jangled keys, and Lee found himself under the ashen, thickening sky, waving as the last car pulled from the curb.

Russell Jarrett, Moira's older brother, stayed longer than the others. He stepped outside carrying a garbage bag.

Lee said, "Those women had a good time today."

"And a few beers. It's worse than a Superbowl party in there."

Lee had returned from Saint Louis a year before, leaving a job teaching eleventh grade history to stay with his mother while she underwent treatment, then when that failed, to care for her as she died. On the day of the funeral, all of it seemed part of another person's life, a story he'd read in the *Caller-Times*. He was thirty-three and now an orphan.

After Russell set the bag on the curb, Lee asked, "Any word from Moira?"

"Flight's delayed," he said. "She'll be here for dinner. She's sorry about missing everything."

Lee hoped Russell would say more but didn't want to press. Moira, he knew, was flying from London where she worked with a dance company, but otherwise her current life remained a mystery. He wondered how England suited her, if she intended to relocate permanently. Except for crossing into Mexico, Lee had never been out of the country—a fact that, like his mother's cancer, he seemed to always be avoiding. He wondered if Moira was traveling alone.

The wind gusted, stripping more leaves from the Chinese tallow. Lee thought to open the windows in the house and start airing out the rooms, then he realized that could be done in an hour or a month; the rushing was over. He said, "I still haven't gone into the den."

"Why should you?" Russell said. "If you need something from there, I'll get it."

"That room doesn't even seem part of the house right now. I can hardly picture it."

Russell untucked his shirt and trained his eyes on a beagle barking down the street. He sold life insurance—he'd written the policy for Lee's mother years before—and regularly interacted with grieving clients, but he was unaccustomed to consoling Lee. For the last three nights, he'd insisted Lee sleep at his apartment, and too often in that time he had guaranteed her insurance papers were in order; he could offer no other relief. Having mentioned the den galled Lee. He'd forgotten his role, had forgotten to chaperone the conversation, because really the day seemed too unremarkable, lacking in weight and ballast, to hold Lee's mother's funeral; the lawn needed raking; browning, discarded Christmas trees lay beside trash cans up and down the street; a tire on her Oldsmobile was flat; Moira, as usual, was late.

Russell had been talking, but Lee heard him say only, "Or maybe you feel relieved. No fault in that."

"I feel hungry." And though he'd meant only to lighten Russell's mood, Lee realized he *was* hungry. It was just past two, the hour when he should've been warming her soup or pouring her cereal.

"They drank the beer, but spared the food," Russell said. "Eat, then take a nap. Try to relax, that's what she would want."

That made sense. Of course he should rest today, yet the idea hadn't occurred to him. Immediately his body started surrendering to the promise of unconsciousness, as if he'd taken one of his mother's sedatives; it was a buoyant feeling, the sense that the worst lay behind him.

Russell said, "When you get up, Moira will be here."

"She'll regale us with stories."

A car with a Christmas wreath tied to its grill turned onto the street, and the driver, a neighbor who hadn't attended the funeral, saluted solemnly.

Lee said, "I think she would've liked the service."

"Absolutely. The flowers, the music, all of her beer-grubbing friends. She'd be proud."

"No," Lee said, "I meant Moira."

MEN COULDN'T GET Moira out of their systems. "Like herpes," she'd once said. For three months after she'd broken a lawyer's heart, he left packages on her porch—flowers, chocolate, a white gold choker, opal earrings; occasionally she'd had to change phone numbers because old flames refused to stop calling. Lee himself could hardly recall a time when he wasn't pining for her. When he had been nothing more than her brother's watchful friend, he'd envied and judged her suitors—young men with long hair and older men with money, a woman who sang jazz, and later, briefly, the singer's husband. His heart thrilled when she dismissed them, though he knew she was beyond him too. Her wispy clothes smelled of marijuana and incense—pungent teases of her other, more essential and alluring life; she made oblique references to a past pregnancy; someone, an affronted spouse or jilted lover, had twice broken her car windows.

The second time was in front of Lee's mother's house. That year, between college and grad school, he'd started finding Moira on his arm, in his bed. He spent nights convincing himself the relationship would last, but Moira left him bewitched and small-feeling, and he always knew she would not grow to need him. The shattered windows evidenced a past and future in which he didn't figure.

A Saturday morning, they stood barefoot on the sun-blanched lawn. Lee's mother had left a note saying she'd gone shopping, but he knew she was at the cemetery, grooming his father's grave.

Moira said, "Everything happens to me twice."

She liked saying this, had said it before. She was referring to jail and lightning; she'd been arrested twice, once for unpaid tickets, once for stealing a mink stole from Dillard's. And twice she'd been struck by lightning, in a sorghum field and beside a pool; she'd been on the early news. Now, the busted windows.

"Things rarely happen to me even once."

"So we're a good fit."

He touched the small of her back, felt the knuckles of her spine. He wondered if his mother had seen the broken glass before leaving, if she'd resisted knocking on his door because she didn't want to spy Moira wrapped in the striped comforter she'd bought him in high school. She viewed Moira as a reckless, wayward flower child and had probably deceived herself into thinking the car belonged to a neighbor.

A joke occurred to him: "Maybe my mother broke them."

"To dissuade me from corrupting her son." She slitted her eyes, smirked darkly. An hour earlier, as his mother washed dishes, Moira'd had to bite the edge of the blanket to muffle her moaning. Now she held the hem of her T-shirt (his actually), threatening to flash the traffic. She liked flashing people.

"We should turn her in."

Looking at the street, Moira said, "The villain always returns to the scene of the crime."

His mother's Oldsmobile eased into the driveway. She cut the ignition (the engine cycled a second or two longer) and lowered the windows an inch. Then she opened the door, said hello, and embraced Moira. Lee watched his mother's eyes close, as if she were receiving adverse news; she didn't look at him. He tried to determine if she'd been crying at the cemetery or if it had been more of an angry morning, but he couldn't tell.

Moira said, "Lee thinks you broke my windows."

His mother eyed the damage, then smiled. She said, "Mama didn't raise no fool son."

They laughed, though Lee felt a rising commotion in his chest. After another glance at the shattered windows, his mother said, "Now, Mr. Detective, grab my groceries from the trunk."

• • •

He had spent Christmas day beside the hospital bed that crowded his mother's small den. He'd adorned the bed's guardrails with red tinsel, but she never noticed. The metastasis had claimed her mind months before, stripped her to a husk of body and voice; in October she'd sobbed and cursed him because he refused to take her trick-or-treating. Now she mostly slept. When she woke Christmas afternoon, he spooned broth into her mouth and wiped her chin. She smiled, then submitted to a sponge bath. Always there was the suppressed, aching hope that such coherence—when she remembered his name or her own, when she spoke lucidly or watched television and not the ceiling fan—signaled some improvement the oncologists could not predict. But when he tried to comb her hair, she screamed; she mistook the brush for a pistol.

A year before, they had driven three hours south and spent the holiday in the Rio Grande Valley and Mexico. They left early to avoid the afternoon heat—even in December temperatures climbed into the nineties. They dallied at rest areas and fruit stands, watched deer graze in the shade of mesquite trees. "Too bad we don't have anything to feed them," she said. Across the border she bought half-priced leather purses and cartons of cigarettes, a sequined serape, and a Santa Claus–shaped piñata for a neighbor's daughter. *Farmacias* anchored almost every corner, and she haggled with girls in dingy lab coats about the prices of muscle relaxers and Procrit. Lee trailed his fingers over the metal shelves where pill bottles were stacked in pyramids; the Spanish labels and dusty surfaces made him feel nervous, illicit. They ate dinner above the Canada Store, and after the enchiladas she drank margaritas—the best she'd ever tasted, she kept saying on the ride home. She was fifty-six. In a week she would start chemo.

"I wonder if it will hurt," she said. "Or if I'll just throw up."

"The doctor said some people don't even get sick. You could be one of those."

She lowered her window, which meant she needed a cigarette. The scratch of her lighter, a flash of flame. He thought she might say something after blowing smoke into the night, but miles ticked by with only the sound of wind slicing around the car. The mucky air smelled of brine, like the Spanish moss draping the trees. Eventually the headlights started illuminating plastic grocery bags caught on barbwire fences.

"Those belonged to illegals," his mother said. She flicked her cigarette outside and rolled up her window. "The bags keep their valuables dry when they cross the river."

She reclined the seat, bent her elbow over her eyes. Though he hadn't realized it was on, Lee could now hear the radio, the speakers whispering an old song, something by the Nitty Gritty Dirt Band. She said, "I wonder what they bring. What would you bring?"

Before he could answer—when he was still imagining the men and women and children fording the river—she said, "I know. You'd take pictures of your girlfriends. And one of Dad. Maybe some books, but they'd get heavy."

"And you. I'd take a picture of you."

She patted his thigh: "Merry Christmas."

"Merry Christmas," he said. He tried tuning the radio, but the reception had faded.

Then she was sitting up, saying, "Daddy was so smart, Lee. He told me about the illegals and their little bags." She shook out another cigarette, lit it, and cranked down her window again. "I thought he was fooling me, lying in the yard like that. I'd brought him water, you know."

He nodded. "I know."

"He'd be so ashamed of me. I've made a mess of everything."

"Don't be silly, Mama," he said. What he believed, though, was that his father would be disappointed, as he himself sometimes was. Since she had run screaming to his father's body years before, she had quit jobs, stripped the walls of his pictures, abandoned her evening walks to sit in the den chain-smoking. Loss had become her religion; in her attempts to conceal her grief, she had worn it the way other women wore wedding rings.

Lee said, "We've had a fine day. You're doing swell. I'm proud of you."

"Leiland, I know what happens." She paused to clear her throat but started hacking hard enough to spill ashes onto the door panel. Her cough was wet and rattling. He cringed, he slowed the car and eased onto the shoulder, but she shook her head and waved him on.

After the spell passed, she said, "I know what happens. I'll lose my hair and vomit and ruin your life. Then I'll still die."

"You're not going to die, Mama," he said. "You'll beat this."

She drew on her cigarette, then let a stream of smoke slip from the side of her mouth. Ahead, a line of cars was backed up at the Sarita check point. The delay would add an hour to the drive, at least.

"Lee," she said, "I don't want to beat it."

HIS MOST RECENT LOVER was a flaxen-haired librarian in Saint Louis, but the relationship had petered out before Lee returned to Corpus. When he'd bought his ticket a year before, he'd thought sheepishly and irrationally of seeing Moira. Then Russell explained about London, the job coordinating rehearsals. For months Lee tried to shut out her presence, but even the glomming heat of the Coastal Bend seemed to share her scent. With Moira he'd always felt his real life was waiting right around the corner, and if he could just keep up she'd lead him to it.

On the night of the funeral, she took a limo to Russell's apartment. "Why take cabs? For ten dollars more you get a town car," she said, then disappeared into the bathroom. Lee had not seen her in five years. A discomposed feeling, almost like fervor, came over him as she showered, but when she emerged wearing baggy jeans and one of Russell's button-downs, he was more relaxed. Moira's hair dripped onto her shoulders, and she looked heavier than he'd remembered. At once, just how often he'd imagined their reunion became clear. The scene had played out countless ways in his mind, yet sitting across from Moira at Russell's table seemed unreal, a dream he couldn't shake after waking. She dribbled the last of the wine into their glasses, and spoke of spending New Year's Eve in a charter plane, flying above fireworks. She said, "They looked like a school of tiny fish or a giant octopus."

"A starving octopus will eat his own heart," Russell blurted. He waggled his glass in a mock toast, his eyes glassy, slow. "I learned that in college."

Moira said, "Russ? Sweetie? How much have you drunk today?"

"Not enough."

"A gang of old women swiped his beer."

"My new year's resolution," Russell said, "is to never fly in a plane with octopi."

Moira cackled, a laugh that started small then opened up and pushed against the dining room walls. Russell seemed unduly offended, so she offered a coy apology. Then she winked at Lee. He said, "My resolution is to find another bottle of wine."

How odd, absurd really, to be looking for chardonnay in Russell's cabinets. After his father's funeral, Lee had spent the night watching his mother sleep in his father's recliner, fearing she'd taken more Valium than she admitted. He woke her every two hours. The vigil afforded the time substance, direction. And since then part of his identity had been attending to her, attempting, even when her health appeared solid, to raise her spirits and assuage her loneliness. He'd invented excuses to call from Missouri, bought airline tickets whenever the prices dropped, counseled her against books and films that might depress her. He couldn't recall not worrying about her, couldn't imagine not worrying in the future. Who was he if not a distant, overprotective son? In Russell's kitchen everything felt random and unmoored. The light seemed too grainy, the creak of the cupboard hinges too shrill. The wine was not where he remembered.

At the table Moira was laughing again. "That's ludicrous, Russell."

"It's true." He smiled drowsily. "Lee, buddy, how tall are you?"

"Five-nine," Lee said, though suddenly the answer seemed wrong, a random number he'd plucked from the ether. "Maybe a little shorter."

Russell shrugged, saying, "Well, you *look* tall."

"Anyway," Moira said, "the short man only paid half price, maybe twenty American dollars. I got in free because I'm a woman, but most men paid forty bucks."

Russell repeated "Forty bucks," chuckling. The alcohol was thickening his tongue, blotching his cheeks.

"What are we talking about?"

"She's regaling us with stories!"

Moira continued, "There were red tube lights hanging from the ceiling, and each room had a sofa, leather or velvet. One had a Jacuzzi. But no doors anywhere. You just walked from room to room, stepping over them." She paused. She glanced at Lee, then Russell, then Lee again. Water trickled in the rain gutter. She said, "People fucking everywhere."

Russell slapped his knee. "Good grief!"

Moira sipped her wine, swallowed quickly. Excitement brightened her eyes. She said, "Waitresses walked around selling chocolate and condoms. I tried not to stare, but that was silly because they *want* you to stare. People you never think of having sex. A deaf woman did sign language to the man on top of her."

"And this place is legal?" Lee asked.

"Completely. It's sleazy and fabulous. You feel—"

"Jesus, Moira," Russell interrupted. He slouched forward, his expression blank. "You didn't."

She narrowed her eyes, then shifted to face the picture window. The night had turned the glass to a mirror, and Lee saw her staring into the darkness. The rain fell heavier now. His mother's plot would be soaked, the sod filling the hole turned to mud. Moira drew her leg up to sit on her calf.

"Of course not, Russell."

They glared at each other for a moment, then Russell refilled his glass. Moira folded her napkin, aligned the edges and smoothed the creases. The heater cycled on.

When no one spoke, Lee asked, "How long can the octopus live without its heart?"

He had been in the front room waiting for the hospice worker to return to the phone, when his mother began calling his name from the den. He was still glum and frustrated from trying to get her to take her morning medication. She'd been feisty, opening and closing her mouth too quickly for him to place the capsule on her tongue, then once he succeeded, she refused to swallow; she smiled and spit the pill onto her nightgown. Eventually she'd co-operated, and when she slept, he crept into the kitchen to arrange delivery of another oxygen canister. It was only October, but November's supply was already exhausted. He'd been on hold for ten minutes, listening to elevator music in the receiver.

"Lee," she called. Her voice was bright but diminished, a sliver of its old self. "Lee."

"Just a minute," he said.

She didn't need help to the bathroom; he'd taken her before her nap. Probably she needed another pack of cigarettes or wanted help lighting one she already had. Recently she'd started forgetting how to smoke. He found her puffing on straws and ballpoint pens, and because it did more good than harm, he left her alone. Withholding her cigarettes allowed him to believe she might live another day, another hour, just as staying on the phone rather than rushing to her side seemed reasonable.

The sound of her fall reminded him of something being dropped into sand. He burst down the hallway, then stopped short of the den's threshold for fear of planting his foot on her body. She wasn't there. His eyes scanned the den—the linen that needed changing, the flowers, the couch and television, her recliner, all of the sharp, hard corners that could hurt her. The room was empty.

Then he saw them; her oxygen tubes pulled taut from the machine, stretching through the sliding doors onto the sundeck. Everything stopped. Through the glass he saw her feet and legs hopelessly tangled in the tubing. The sun shone bright on her body, illuminating pale, dry thighs. Her left hand still clutched her nightgown. He pictured her inching toward the deck, holding the hem above her ankles so she wouldn't stumble. A cigarette and her lighter lay a few feet away. His heart flattened: blood. It saturated a lock of her hair and dripped down to collect in a spreading, syrupy puddle. She was not crying or speaking or doing anything at all; her eyes were locked on the potted azalea in front of her.

"Mama," he said, trying to calm the panic in his voice. "Mama, are you okay?"

When she didn't answer, he thought *this is how it happened, this is where you found her.* Months before, they had come onto the sundeck when her hair started falling out, and he shaved her head, first with clippers, then a razor. She had said she felt like a recruit going to boot camp.

"Mama," he said. "Mama, it's Lee."

She blinked, then blinked again, and smacked her lips, as if just waking. He exhaled. The world resumed its motion. She smiled and lifted her dull, wet eyes to him.

She said, "Trick or treat."

ON THE NIGHT of the funeral Lee decided to sleep at home. Moira drove him because she wanted to pick up a pint of ice cream. She sped through the slick streets, rifling through a box of cassettes with one hand. They could've been years in the past, stealing away from Russell to find a bar or camp on Bird Island, or skip everything and go straight to bed. The familiarity relieved and vexed him. A solemn tingling ran along his nerves, a building anticipation as if she were driving him into an undiscovered country. Along Ocean Drive the bay looked like petroleum, and the sprawling homes were still strung with Christmas lights. Luminaria lit one sidewalk; Moira had once told him how she used to kick them over on Christmas Eve.

She placed the cassettes in the backseat. She'd found nothing. "Who needs a soundtrack?"

"Not us," he said.

They stopped at a traffic signal. The glow of the red light tinted Moira's face. She said, "Actually I fucked a man in Amsterdam. At that swingers' club. Was that obvious at the table?"

"No," he said. He blew into his hands. The engine idled, a loose screw vibrated in the dash. He expected the signal to turn green, but it didn't, and he saw her under the tube lights, under the faceless man. "No, you fooled us."

She nodded distractedly. The light stayed red, but the road was abandoned and after a moment she accelerated through the intersection.

"I didn't intend to," she said. "He just had such, I don't know, *certainty*. Mostly I remember his skin tasting metallic, he probably worked with steel. Not really my type, but who knows, maybe we loved each other for a few minutes."

"We would have to know what love is to know that," Lee said. The words sounded confident and mysterious, even romantic, which he liked, though he'd never considered them before. He spoke differently around Moira, always had.

She parked behind his mother's Olds and cut the ignition. The headlights stayed beaming on the bumper and a single streetlamp distinguished the small houses of the neighborhood. She said, "You're sure you don't want ice cream?"

"I'm fine." After saying this, he wondered why he'd answered that way.

Rain drummed on the hood, streaked and pilled the windows. As he reached for the door, she said, "It must have been a nightmare."

For days those words had hovered in conversations, but no one had said them straight out. They made him feel caught in a lie. Moira bit her lip. In the dimness she looked forlorn and exhausted, years older than she was. He suddenly longed to console her. He almost admitted that every time he'd seen his mother's car since her death, and even when she was still breathing but dull and relegated to the hospital bed, the words *She's home* scrolled through his mind. He heard them, even envisioned the letters, and his heart stuttered. The words had come when he came from Russell's to dress for the funeral, when they had returned to the house afterward. *She's home. She's home.* He considered telling Moira that the words had come just moments earlier when she steered into the driveway and killed the engine.

He said nothing. If he'd spoken he would have wept, and leaning across the seat he realized weeping terrified him. Moira no longer reeked of incense, but he smelled her perfume, maybe the same musky scent a woman had worn that morning, maybe one his mother had stocked when she sold Avon. At first her mouth stayed tight, and for an extended, desperate moment he feared she would recoil and push him away. But soon she touched his face and let him taste the wine on her tongue, let him breathe her warm breath. She moaned, a soft whimpering that made him self-conscious, like a teenager worried his parents were spying out the window; the moaning exhilarated him too. Moira's jacket rustled when he pulled her closer. He pressed his face to her neck; he inhaled her. He listened to her breathing, to her voice saying *Take me inside;* he listened to the cars on the road, to their tires hissing like fireworks before they explode into light.

"WHAT'S THE CRUELEST thing you've ever done?" Moira had asked years before. They were parked outside the fence at Cabaniss Field, at the end of the runway, watching planes practice touch-and-go landings. They had been together for a few months, and lately she'd been posing such questions. She especially liked to ask him after they made love, "Have you ever *really* broken someone's heart? What's the blackest lie you've told? What's your most depraved fantasy?" Then because the questioning seemed to give her such a charge, they usually rolled around again. He'd never answered in earnest, afraid what he had to offer would betray his inexperience. At twenty-six he had no secrets worth keeping. Nor had he ever gathered the courage to turn the questions back on Moira, knowing that at twenty-two, she had plenty.

The lights of a single-engine turboprop appeared in the sky, descending toward the landing strip.

"Or no, what's the cruelest thing you *would do*?"

"Depends."

"Would you hurt someone if he didn't deserve it?"

"Of course not."

"What if I asked you to? Or your mother did?"

"You wouldn't. She wouldn't."

"Say we did. Say we wanted you to really hurt someone, and the only reason we wanted you to was to prove that you would."

The plane grew nearer, a darker patch of dark in the charcoal sky. His mother was home watching the Lifetime Movie Network.

"Yes," he said, "I would."

Moira fixed her eyes on the runway, smiling slyly, obliquely. She reached across the seat, found his hand and pulled it to her lap. At first he thought she'd taken hold of him because he'd snowed her into believing he was capable of that which he wasn't; now her tightening grip, her sweating palm, even the lights on the plane's wings, showed she didn't believe a single lie he'd told.

A week later, walking in Heritage Park, she told him she was leaving, that there was someone else.

"Who?" he asked.

"I don't know yet."

A WEEK AFTER CHRISTMAS, Lee found his mother gasping short, high-pitched breaths. He'd fallen asleep on the couch in the den, and when he woke he switched on a lamp, expecting to see her crying. She wasn't. Her eyes were glazed and bleary, fixed on the ceiling. He checked the oxygen tubes for kinks, adjusted the cannula in her nose. He ran warm water over a washcloth, then blotted her forehead. He wiped her cheeks and limp, listless arms. He asked her to squeeze his hand or blink, but she stayed still, her breathing sharp as blades.

At four in the morning their hospice nurse, a stout Mexican man named Tony, answered after one ring. Tejano music played in the background. Lee detailed his mother's day; soggy cereal for lunch and two diaper changes; she had slept most of the afternoon and evening but was current on her pills; the catheter bag was half full; he could not remember the last time she had spoken. Tony asked him to lower the phone so he could hear her breathing. Lee held the receiver close to his mother's mouth and wondered how long she had been in this condition. He wondered if she'd called for him while he slept.

A coma, or similar to one. Her lungs, Tony said, were filling with fluid that had leaked through the membranes, a result of protein depletion. He said lungs are like sponges and when saturated, air cannot penetrate them. He said he'd expected this — Lee realized Tony had turned off the Tejano music — and was surprised it hadn't happened sooner. In the den, her ventilator whirred. On the phone a distant nighttime static buzzed. Tony apologized.

He told Lee to place a morphine tablet under his mother's tongue and dissolve it with water from a straw. The pill would relax her, take pressure off her lungs, though soon her breathing would likely slow to such a degree that it would completely cease. Her body was shutting down. Tony said he was coming over, but he lived across the bay in Portland so the drive would take half an hour. Lee told his mother not to worry and turned on the television so she wouldn't feel alone while he went to the kitchen. He found the pills and poured water into a glass. He took one of the crazy straws that she liked and returned to the den. He smiled in case she could see.

He spoke to his mother as if she were a child. He pried her mouth open while her eyes stared vacantly forward. Her tongue was pasty, rigid. Her breath smelled oniony. Her jaws clenched, making a muffled chewing noise. When he held them open, the high-pitched breathing became a strained groaning. He relented. He closed his eyes, forced himself to breathe. *Please*, he thought, *please*. After a moment he opened her mouth again. She bit him. Then again. Then he lifted her tongue, held it awkwardly with his finger, and positioned the tablet. He leaned over to suck water into the straw, then trapped it with his thumb on the top. Once released into her mouth, the water dribbled down her chin and drained into her throat. Liquid gurgled in her chest. Her body coughed. Then she lay still. Lee opened her mouth and saw the tablet, still dry. He drew water into the straw again, set it directly on top of the tablet and watched its edges effervesce. He climbed into the bed. Through all of this, he talked to her. Tony had said, "Let her know you're there. She can hear you, and she's scared."

He complimented her and he lied; he spoke of his father, because suddenly he understood she'd want to hear of him. He recalled for her the months his father had spent beneath his old Subaru, reversing the transmission's gear configuration just to see if it would work; the time they had tubed down the Frio River and the current kept pulling Dad into the weeds so that finally he followed them on the far bank; his singsong way of answering the phone. Lee spoke calmly, and hearing his own voice, he realized his mother's life was ending in these very moments. He turned off the television. He put his arm around her shoulder, cradled the fragility of her bone, flesh. He asked her questions then answered them. When he ran out of things to say, he cleared his throat and began singing.

He sang "Amazing Grace" in a near whisper, like a lullaby. Her teeth began to grind, and she started groaning again. Her head lolled, her fingers twitched. Her dry, peeling lips lost color. Lee sang louder, ashamed to realize his voice had a pleasing resonance, a warm reverberation buoying his tone. He started and abandoned and returned to different verses without thinking. The harsh, labored panting began to taper. He kept singing. He did not let his voice waver but concentrated on maintaining a clean, even pitch, for slipping off key seemed unpardonable. His mother's breathing calmed further. He sang, sang, sang. And when her lungs finally and quietly gave in, when her fingers went still and her jaw relaxed, he kept singing as he pulled the quilt to her shoulders and closed her eyes with his hand. He stayed beside her while the world rushed away. He plummeted through an opening emptiness, his body surrendering as if the earth and gravity were receding. He floated through nights on Russell's couch and through the funeral, and he kept floating until he landed in his bed with Moira.

The rain came harder as he moved inside her. She straddled him, and he touched her eyelids, her mouth, neck, breasts. Her skin was milk blue in the night. He fought to remember each time they'd made love before, entrusted her to envelop and consume him, like the rain outside, like the ocean, to make him feel as she had years earlier, to say his name and remind him who he was.

Moira held his face with her warm, trembling hands. She said, "It's okay."

She draped her arm and leg across his body. Headlights from a line of cars cut through the window of Lee's room, then she rolled onto her back and said, "Ice cream turns my stomach."

"Not your average pillow talk."

"I wanted to drive you. I didn't want you to be alone." She sat up, bunched the sheets around her. Her hair shone as she stared out the window. Lee felt his heart beating. She said, "Maybe I made a mistake. Do you wish this hadn't happened?"

"I kept thinking of you. When it was happening, I couldn't stop." As he said this, as he wished he hadn't said anything, he realized it was true. Holding his mother, when he owed her his strictest attention as he owed her his life itself, he'd been unable to keep Moira at bay. Just on the other side of the moment, she was biting her bottom lip, playing pool; she was dousing her eggs with Tabasco sauce; she carried a baker's rack down the stairs when Russell moved into his apartment, carried it because they'd said she couldn't; she was tussling with him in the mornings, teaching him the beauty of occasional sexual stillness, and he was resting his cheek on her stomach afterward. As soon as she had come to Lee years earlier—he'd never been so deluded to think he'd pursued and caught her—he'd started waiting for her to leave. But when his mother was dying, his heart had leapt because he knew Moira would come back.

She ran her fingers through her hair. He caressed her flesh, the curvature of her ribs and the space between the bones, then he let his hand fall to the bed. A kaleidoscope of memories swirled: how, massaging his mother's back, he always waited for the first moment she kindly said he could stop; how after he'd taken her for a Demerol injection at the ER, she'd blissfully said, "From now on I'm going to do better"; how before the local tremors took over her hands, she'd been delighted for days by crayons and coloring books. Now he felt wistfully desperate, as he had when Moira had been prone to asking her grave questions. What would she ask tonight? He imagined his furtively beautiful answers, imagined them arousing her and delivering the two of them into another sweating tangle of limbs. More than anything he wanted another chance. Below his longing was a whirling disgust for having spoken of his mother, for drawing the comparison that would remind Moira of the night's gravity and rekindle, whether by guilt or kindness, the ruthless passion he so desired.

She climbed on top of him again, placed her hands above his shoulders. Sweat glazed her skin. She said, "I'm so sorry."

He smiled and raised himself to kiss her. She let him, but that was all. She tucked her hair behind her ears, then lowered to her elbows and began stroking his face, peering at him in the near dark. Again she whispered, "I'm sorry." She pressed her cheek to his, then lay beside him, her body relaxed. Years before, in Heritage Park when she had claimed both to love him and no longer love him, when he begged her to stay and knew she wouldn't, he'd felt the same dread. He listened to her easy breathing, listened until it quieted. On her hip he felt a tiny half-moon of raised flesh. Possibly the scar had been there for years and his greedy fingers had never noticed it, but he suspected the wound was more recent, the consequence of a mundane miscalculation, a timely slip on wet pavement or a hard pivot into an open kitchen drawer. Such a small thing, but it intimated the trajectory of Moira's coming life: soon she would be working in an office, a dour job to help with a mortgage; she'd be married to a kindly, complacent man; she'd be pregnant. If she remembered this night, the memory would be fleeting—a last example of who she thought she'd become. Lee's presence was arbitrary. He knew this as surely as he knew she'd be gone before sunrise. Her lungs filled and emptied, and when she was immersed in the steady rhythm of sleep, he crept out of the room.

The den still stunk of cigarettes and talcum. The odor hollowed him. Moonlight slanted through the blinds; the rain had stopped. He lay in her hospital bed, naked and shivering, and covered himself with her quilt, which smelled of the petroleum jelly he'd rubbed on her cracked lips. He had the distinct sensation of being borne toward a cliff. His thoughts went not to his mother—but to the women at the funeral, to Russell, and to Moira, for suddenly—keenly, terribly—what they had understood all along became clear: this was only the beginning. Nothing would estrange him from the rootlessness ahead. Fits of sobbing would seize him when he least expected, in traffic and the shower, in the grocery and two years later in his Saint Louis classroom—and tonight as he clutched the bed's guardrails and clung to the red tinsel his mother had never seen. He would hold on too long. Then he was swept over the edge and weeping for all of them, weeping like a man who was dying or a newborn child, blind and terrified and gasping for breath.

His mother had soaked in a bath after they returned from Mexico. When she stepped into the den, she smelled of soap and steam. She situated herself in the recliner and said, "I'm sorry I got upset in the car. Maybe I drank too many margaritas, but they were so good."

He lay on the couch watching the late news. The Santa piñata stood atop the television. He said, "Water under the bridge."

"Did you talk to Russell? Did he have a nice holiday?"

He nodded, though he hadn't spoken with him at all. Russell

would have asked about their trip, about her health and spirits, and Lee would have been obligated to contrive hopeful, winsome answers. Tonight he lacked the energy for such condolences.

"Don't appease me," she said, unwrapping a pack of cigarettes, "but I'd like to hear what you remember about the old holidays. That's fair on Christmas." She blew a plume of smoke into the air. "Don't tell me about sneaking into your presents. We knew about that."

"You did?"

"Don't ever become a thief. You don't hide things very well," she said. "Tell me something else. I won't get upset."

Immediately, as if he'd been awaiting the opportunity, he said, "I used to lie awake listening to you and Dad set out the gifts. You always wanted them arranged a certain way."

She laughed a little laugh, then stayed smiling. "I did, I did."

"I'd wait until you had everything perfect, then pretend to wake up. I made noise to warn you."

She turned to the window; the tip of her cigarette glowed orange when she inhaled. A wave of guilt swamped him. Maybe all of their Christmases blurred and conflated in her mind, but more probably she remembered what he hadn't mentioned, what in his fatigue he'd not thought to avoid. On at least one of those mild December mornings—though over the years he suspected it was their annual tradition—she and his father made love after arranging the presents. From his room Lee had heard their muffled voices in the hall, heard their bedroom door easing closed and bodies sinking into a mattress. After they opened gifts, his parents shared cigarettes. His childhood seemed a haze of bluish smoke. He could not recall what his mother had looked like then, though he could imagine her as a child, opening her own gifts. She was a wistful girl who would never want college or money, just a husband to care for her, a child she could care for. Maybe tonight she felt she'd wanted too much.

"You have a good memory," she said. "I do too. It's not always a blessing."

"No," he said, "I guess not."

She stubbed out her cigarette, then lay back in the recliner. She said, "I'm sorry you're going to remember all of this, all of what's coming. It's not fair."

By rote, he began, "We just need to—"

"Don't say anything, Lee," she interrupted. "I'm okay tonight. I'm optimistic."

She pulled up the quilt, raised her knees so her feet rested on the cushion. She was trying to keep her eyes open, and though he wanted to encourage her before she drifted off, to thank and exalt her, he said nothing. Ever so slightly his heart had started to cave in and render him silent. Her hopefulness was igniting his own fear, enlivening the almost tangible sense of despair he struggled constantly to suppress. When he looked again, her eyes were lidded and she was breathing peacefully; he lowered the volume on the television, so she wouldn't wake. If the night could relieve them of the day, he believed the morning would find him rejuvenated, replenished.

"Maybe optimistic is wrong," she said, suddenly awake. "Maybe tomorrow I'll be gloomy, but I think we'll survive this. Next Christmas we'll drink margaritas in Mexico. You can bring Russell, maybe that little sister of his if she's here, and this will all seem like a bad dream. Won't that be nice?"

He couldn't answer. Her lighter snapped, the fragrance of smoke wafted. He sensed her staring at him but closed his eyes and stayed quiet. As his mother waited for his familiar, reassuring voice, he rolled over and pretended to sleep.

Gift Wrap

by Lynne Barrett

This year the store *Paper, Ink* has set up a kiosk out front, in its hip block of shops, and Jen works there all day wrapping. You bring in your present with your receipt from one of the stores and get a discount. It's part of the strategy for reviving this old beach town's center. She uses muted, cool, shimmery papers and French wire ribbons. She does each gift with care, choosing among the trims she made ahead—seashells and starfish sprayed silver, the Florida equivalent of snowflakes.

When she began, shoppers would watch her, then go into the store to buy supplies to do the work themselves, but now, two days before Christmas, they have abandoned such ambitions. Today some even come with presents bought elsewhere and pay full price. She is astonished at how much money other people have to throw away.

A young guy places three identical jewelry boxes on her counter. She asks how he wants her to mark which is whose. "No," he confides, "I got them all the same, ankle bracelets, no mistakes. They're for my girlfriends." He says this ruefully, with a flash of dark eyes. As she twists out a chrysanthemum bow, he says, "You have beautiful hands," such a flirt she knows how easily he's keeping three women on the hook. She remembers when she was single and had time to be miserable.

Now she has a sweet husband, Carlos, and a son, Riley, six, so beautiful her heart twists each time she sees him. Her father has been with them since the weekend, and right about now he's picking up her sister at the airport. Her mother died last June, and for the first time Jen is the home base for the holiday. Her mother made a big deal of Christmas—too big, Jen always thought, full of such effort and dressing up, no one could relax. She misses her mother, but she definitely doesn't want to be like her.

At half past five, just as she's closing, her sister arrives. Haley is younger, taller, blonder, and richer than Jen. That's always her first impression, Haley's vitality, before her discontent comes through. She works eighty hours a week marketing technology. Haley's phone calls are a cascade of promotions, raises, moving expenses to new states, last month a vacation to Australia. She has friendships on the Internet and no sign of any permanent connections.

"Dad's parking," Haley says. "Riley's with him. He's so cute. I haven't seen him since the funeral."

Jen asks Haley to help her carry in the supplies and introduces her to the other women from the shop. Haley is pleasant till they get outside again. Then she says, "Riley says you didn't make the lebkuchen."

Jen sighs. She knew there would be trouble if she didn't make those cookies. Haley sent her the recipe in November, even though Jen already had it, and a set of cutters just like their mother's. "Listen, this is what I'm doing," Jen says. "Carlos got this smoker and he's smoking a goose. I'm making light stuff. We're having a fruit salad and pumpkin risotto and green beans and some good bread.

And mango ice cream for dessert because that's Riley's favorite. He wouldn't even eat the lebkuchen last year. He doesn't like food to be crunchy. Okay?"

"No mashed potatoes?" her sister says. "No squash?"

Jen sighs. "No. And no minced pie."

"Okay, but there have to be lebkuchen," her sister says.

"I got the ingredients, Haley, but I just didn't have time," Jen says. "They take all day, you know that. I've been working extra hours, and I've had Dad here. Give me a break."

"Lebkuchen are traditional in our family," Haley says. "Our great-grandmother made them."

"Sometimes you have to start new traditions," Jen says.

Haley doesn't answer. She has a stubborn sulky look Jen knows well, the one she wore when she wanted something from their mother.

"Mom made all that stuff last year," Jen says, "when she shouldn't have."

Last year at Christmas, their mother knew she was sick. She didn't tell them till after the dinner, after the huge ridiculous turkey and mashed potatoes and creamed onions and the big sticky trifle no one ate. Last year—the sisters look at each other and veer away. Riley runs up to them, towing his grandfather.

"You're right," Haley says. But she doesn't sound convinced.

JEN AND CARLOS have a small blue deco house in an old neighborhood on the rise. It has a fireplace, a little turret, hardly any closets, and no guest room. When they get home she puts her sister's two big suitcases in the narrow Florida room, where there's a futon. Her dad has been sleeping there, but now he'll bunk in with Riley.

After dinner they all decorate the small tree with her collection of birds, Guatemalan and Moravian doves, origami cranes, sequinned peacocks, lovebirds of spun glass. They top it with a paper partridge in a nest of gold shreds Riley made when he was with her at work after school last week. Then she lets her sister read to Riley and put him to bed.

When she goes in to kiss him goodnight, after doing the dishes, Haley is telling him how their great-grandmother came from Alsace as a small girl, her father a baker. "Lebkuchen was their recipe," Haley says, looking at Jen. "It's from the word *lieb*, love. It means love cookie."

"Do you remember them from last year?" Jen asks him. Riley sleepily shakes his head no.

When Jen was Riley's age her great-grandmother was still alive—a hefty woman with gray braids pinned up around her head in a crown and the most wonderful cheeks, ruddy and curved. Riley's cheeks have that same shape right now. And so Jen yields. "I guess we could make them tomorrow," she says to Haley. "But you'll have to do most of the work."

Her dad—Riley McGraw, Big Riley he wants to be called now—has happily gone to seed since her mother's death. Up in Newport News, he fished all summer and never cleaned the house. This week, when Jen sent him out for groceries, he found a neighborhood bar she didn't know existed, a cubbyhole where the owner,

Ed, is a great guy, her dad says. They were in the same navy, same ocean. Now her dad asks if he can invite Ed for Christmas dinner. What can she say but yes? And his girlfriend, her dad adds, the barmaid, a great gal. They'll bring something to eat.

Later, as they collapse into bed, she tells Carlos it's all too much. "Next year," he says, "we'll find someplace to take everybody out." Carlos was raised by his aunt who brought him from Argentina. She died while he was in college. Everyone but Jen calls Carlos Chuck, he's the most American guy you've ever seen, and he rarely talks about the past. After her mother's death he wept in big coughing groans. For that, among other things, she'll love him forever.

"You add the baking soda to the mix of molasses and sugar and spices and lard and it all fizzes up. That's the fun part," her sister says. Riley, in his striped pj's, sits on a stool, watching seriously.

"Now the egg yolk. Then you sift in flour a cup at a time." Haley sifts while Jen stirs.

"I just barely remember when our grandmother made these," Jen says. "You were a baby then, Haley."

"The earliest I remember is Grandma's house. She lived in the mountains," Haley tells Riley, "in a big old house."

"Everyone would gather. There were so many women—two different Aunt Mildreds, and Grandma, and Mom, and Aunt Judy who used to be married to our Uncle Bob. And more, some cousins, who were very old."

"They'd put the dough in a crock and set it outside to chill overnight."

"We're going to have to put it in the fridge—God, there's a lot of it, Haley."

"And this is the half recipe—"

"It needs to chill till it's hard. And then we'll roll it out and cut it. Here are the cutters—you can play with them, Riley, they're not sharp. After you bake them and they cool, you ice them."

Her arm aches. Jen hands off to Haley, turns to make coffee. She can hear her father moving around in the bathroom. Carlos left for work early.

"So there's a story Mom told us," Haley says.

"Tell me," Riley says.

"Well, it seems that our mom and dad got engaged just before Christmas one year, and then, when all the women were making the lebkuchen, she was helping and she noticed after they'd made the dough—"

"I think it was after the rolling out," says Jen.

"No, it was after making the dough—after it had been put outside and turned into a big frozen lump, as I heard it. Anyway, Mom noticed that she'd lost her engagement ring."

"This old tale," her father says as he comes into the kitchen.

"Well, they looked all over. The other women had put their rings in a teacup before they started, but Mom was so proud of her new ring, she hadn't wanted to take it off." Haley shook her arm, stretched. "And they realized it must be in the dough."

Jen takes over. The dough is almost too stiff to stir. "So they looked for it when they made the cookies, but they didn't see it," Jen says. "And then as everyone ate them they had to be really careful because a diamond could crack your teeth, you know."

"What are you talking about?" her dad says. "Those lebkuchen are so hard they can break teeth all on their own. That's how I lost mine," he says and pops out his partial plate, to Riley's delight.

"Oh, Dad," says Haley. "Just 'cause it's not your family recipe."

"My mother made fruitcake," he says. Haley and Jen roll their eyes at each other. Nobody liked that fruitcake, gummy and stiff.

"Let me finish the story," Jen says. "So guess who bit into a cookie and found it?"

"Who," says Riley. "Did you, Mom?"

"No, no, I wasn't born yet."

"Not even thought of," their dad says. "Your mother wasn't the type."

Jen and Haley laugh at their dad, the rogue.

"No, Mary found it. That's your grandmother," he says to Riley. "She ate nothing but lebkuchen all Christmas Day, she was so determined not to let that ring be lost down anyone's gullet."

"Which shape cookie was it in?" asks Riley.

His grandfather looks over the Santa, the bell, the Christmas tree, the moon, the star, and the gingerbread boy. "It was in the moon. And that's why, your grandmother said, the moon always tastes the best."

• • •

LATER, HER FATHER, alone with her, says, "You know, that bit with the ring didn't happen to your mom, but to your Aunt Judy, when she was your uncle's fiancée."

"What do you mean? Mom always told it to us this way."

"Well, as I recall it happened to Judy, and then when Judy left the family, in the divorce, I think your mother sort of adopted it. You couldn't let such a fun story go just because of a little divorce."

"I can't believe that. Really? Are you just teasing me?"

"Your mother had her ideas," he says, looking so sad all of a sudden that Jen lets it go.

CHRISTMAS EVE. She wraps umbrellas, diving gear, breakable bowls, designer toothbrushes. Lotions with the smell of carnations and rain. People are humming, people are crazed.

She has the feeling that all her indomitability, all her thought and skill and work, are being poured into things that don't get anywhere, don't mount up. They're like this wrapping she's doing, lavished with her talent only to be torn apart tomorrow and tossed out.

When she gets home, Carlos is drinking a beer in the backyard and watching Riley chase lizards. "She's sent me to Publix, twice," Carlos says. "On Christmas Eve. She needed more baking sheets, and then waxed paper and containers to put the cookies in, after. And I had to take the battery out of the smoke detector—it kept going off."

"I'm sorry," Jen says. "Hey, Riley, how come you're not helping Aunt Haley?"

"I did," he says, "but I got tired. Look Mom, my tooth is loose."

And he wiggles his lower left front tooth till it sticks out at a wild angle. Already? She has a pang. It's all going to happen to him— loss, change, death. She knows she must be tired, to leap from a loose tooth to her son's mortality.

She gathers her strength and pushes through a wall of gingery heat into the kitchen. Haley's hair is in her face. "Your kitchen is small," Haley says accusingly.

"Hi, honey—I'll help you in a minute." Jen walks into the bedroom and closes the door. She changes into a T-shirt and shorts, pulls her hair back, and takes a deep breath before she goes out to bake.

"It must be a hundred degrees in here," Haley says, pulling a hot tray out.

"At least. Florida's no place for this kind of cooking. I told you that."

"You know what," Haley says, "I don't need this. I've been working for hours, just trying to make something nice—" Her voice breaks.

"You're just like Mom," Jen says. "You want everything to be a big production." She tries to say it lightly, but it comes out with a sting.

"I'm not the one," says Haley. "It's you. You have to have your own ideas about how everything's supposed to be, all new and different and artsy—"

"Okay, fine. At least in her own home," Jen dumps shortening on the next sheet right over the greasy crumbs, "Mom got to do things her way."

"Humph," grunts Haley, a sound so precisely like their mother in her Christmas snit that Jen wants to laugh.

And then, to her horror, as she fits lebkuchen on the baking sheet, she humphs too. Maybe it's a German noise, she thinks, old as Father Christmas and the spice cookies themselves, an ancient female sound of solstice effort.

"It's so hard to believe she's gone," Haley says, and the sisters work on through a glaze of tears.

Two hundred cooling cookies fill the house. Her dad has picked up pizza, and they eat it in the yard.

Jen puts Riley to bed and almost falls asleep beside him, soothed by his even breathing. She and Carlos go about their final Christmas Eve tasks while Haley mutters over the icing. She covers the dining room table with waxed paper and lays the cookies out on it.

Jen sways, looking at her. Where does her sister get the energy?

"Go to bed," Haley says, unexpectedly tender. "I have it under control. You were right—these are too much to do."

"Maybe a quarter recipe?" Jen sticks her finger in the icing, already hardening.

"You need a team of women."

"Women who have time," Jen agrees.

Christmas morning is warm, shiny. Jen is the first up, leaving Carlos snoring. Her father lies in a sleeping bag by Riley's bed, surrounded by stuffed animals, with his teeth out. Riley is cuddled next to him. Haley, on the futon, is tousled, groggy, young.

Jen plugs in the lights and the tree glitters, all the birds flocked upon it, presents mounded underneath. Hers (beautiful pens for the adults, an easel and art set for Riley) are wrapped in silver and purple, Carlos's done in funny papers he saved up. Haley's gifts make a pile of traditional green and red. Her father's, in foil bags, are clearly bottles. Santa—very hip—left presents wrapped in white tissue rubber-stamped with hot pink reindeer. She sits enjoying the way it all shimmers until the others get up, thinking how her mother must have felt, last Christmas, trying to make something lavish before she left them.

Then, in their pajamas, her family opens everything in a binge of rip and ooh.

And the day actually goes something like she'd imagined. They hang around and play with Riley's new kangaroo and joey puppets and world habitats puzzle and the whoopee cushion from his grandfather, while the goose smokes. The rest of the dinner is easily made. Her dad's buddy Ed shows up with his girlfriend, Emilia, who brings a *paneton*, traditional, she says, at home in Lima. "Somewhat like fruitcake," her dad says, "but cakier," and then Carlos says, "It's what my aunt used to serve for dessert on Christmas, always with cocoa."

So their Christmas dessert is mango ice cream, lebkuchen, hot chocolate, and *paneton*. The lebkuchen are thicker than normal. "I probably didn't roll them out enough. I was trying to go fast," Haley says.

They lack that crisp snap, but they're delicious, better in fact, altogether more Southern and yielding. Jen tastes more molasses, less clove. And Riley is already halfway through a moon.

That Clapton Christmas

by Michael Parker

That was the Christmas of Shelly Phillips, my first big-time crush, whom I'd bought a brown suede choker for Christmas. In return she'd given me a 45 of King Floyd singing "Groove Me: And I know you're gonna groove me, baby." That's what I was trying to talk to Shelly Phillips about.

Shelly and I had to exchange gifts early because it was my family's turn to head over to Saint Paul's that Christmas to spend the day with the McCormicks, cousins on our mother's side. We alternated traveling to our cousins, and they to us, on Thanksgiving and Christmas. They'd come over for Thanksgiving, so now it was our turn to drive the little-over-an-hour-depending-on-which-route-you-took to Saint Paul's. I liked my cousins—three boys close to me in age—and I didn't so much mind it once we arrived at their house. But I did not want to go that Christmas. For one thing I'd planned on getting together later on with Shelly Phillips, and I was fourteen and even though I had yet to read my Schopenhauer I understood very well the notion that the world was nothing more than an extension of my will.

Also I hated traveling on Christmas Day. It was then, is now, the most melancholy travel time of the year. Often in December in eastern North Carolina, the only thing vaguely white on the ground is the jaundiced yellow of fallow roadside fields. I've spent many a Christmas afternoon sweating in shirt sleeves. Our '68 Ford Country Squire station wagon crammed with the seven of us (my parents in the front, my older brothers and sisters in the back, my youngest sister and I stretched out in the Very Back) was fresh-airless and smelled of my oldest brother's hands, which inevitably, year-round, reeked of peanut butter. It being Christmas morning, there was nothing good on the radio, so we could not even distract ourselves with the obligatory fight over which AM station to tune into: WKIX, which favored Top 40 of the Gary Puckett and the Union Gap or Motown variety, or WPTF, which broadcast a show my father liked called *Ask Your Neighbor,* an on-air yard sale featuring buyers and sellers from the entire coastal plain hawking mostly incomprehensible agricultural and industrial wares like manure spreaders and paint mixers.

Nor was there much to look at outside. There were few cars on the road, the ones present slow-motion coasting. Country people, notorious for rising early, seemed abed still, or already at church. The parking lots of Mount Moriah Baptist and Philadelphia AME Zion were filling up. Church, steeple, but where were all the people? From the backward glance of the Very Back, the world in reverse looked very *Twilight Zone.* I watched the occasional blur of a kid trying out a new toy—a lucky boy on a Honda 75 bumping over the furrows of a roadside field or a girl in a driveway choppily pedaling a pink banana bike, her grandmama posted sentry on the steps of the ranch house, smoking away glumly at a cigarette I could tell from fifty miles an hour was extra long and extravagantly unashed.

There were two routes from Clinton, my hometown, to Saint Paul's. The Front Way followed the main highways, 24 to Fayetteville then on to I-95 for the final dozen miles. The Front Way featured more distractions: a small grocery store hard after the bridge over the muddy Cape Fear River called the Hoggily Woggily, a play on the chain of Piggly Wigglies dominating Clinton and a joke I never seemed to tire of; the quick and dead hamlets of Autryville and Steadman; the sleazy outskirts of what we'd taken to calling Fayette Nam, a town back then given generously to providing vice to soldiers returning from the war.

My father hated the interstate. He liked the Back Way. The problem was it took longer, and the countryside seemed malevolent that Christmas morning. The fields straggled sullen and muddy alongside us; wintry trees lined them, smudgy gray and sinister in the distance. The only landmark of distinction was a middle-of-nowhere house with a two-story porch made of lattice, painted yellow. For obvious reasons this house appealed to the most wistful region of my imagination. I wanted inside it during a gold-plated sunset, wanted the diamond patterns to fall on the bare shoulders of Shelly Phillips. *In a great big latticed porch, all you got to do is groove me, baby. Make me feel good inside.*

The House of Yellow Lattice was not enough to quell the

stultifying quarters of the Very Back. Halfway or earlier, my sister and I started to kick each other. Shouts from the back, admonitions from the front, the smell of hot metal, peanut butter, and red dust. I could not wait to get out of that car, even in Saint Paul's.

Which, being half the size of Clinton, a paltry seven thousand itself, was open season for blink-and-you'll-miss-it, lone-stoplight quips. When I think of the collective sarcasm of five reasonably intelligent, ironically inclined kids—when I compare it to the acid-edged repartee of my single daughter, in comparison so relatively benign—I don't understand why my parents did not stop at a bridge over a swamp on the Back Way and drown us all like a sack of unwanted puppies.

But they kept us around, and we kept up our more-cosmopolitan-than-thou insults. You'd think one dusty eastern North Carolina town would be about the same as the next, but even the presence of a Hardee's or a Dairy Queen is enough to justify pretensions. Saint Paul's was so dead it appeared freeze framed. I was shocked to see dogs roaming the sidewalks, leaves unleashed by a breeze, the blink of a time/temp bank sign.

My cousins lived dead center of Saint Paul's deadness, in a twenties bungalow that made our fifties ranch house seem straight out of the *Jetsons*. The ceilings were high; the plaster was bulging; the bedrooms opened into each other, dark and stuffy, like diseased internal organs; you had to pass through at least one to get to the bathroom, a situation which seemed to a fourteen-year-old like myself, fourth of five children, in pursuit at all times of a little impossibly earned privacy, hellish.

My cousins didn't seem to notice the unfortunate layout. They were always happy to see us. That Clapton Christmas we treated them terribly. Out of the car, into the house, hey to Uncle Bill, hugs to Aunt Dot, and we'd disappear into the front bedroom shared by Neil and Mark, wherein lay the treasure: hundreds of comics our cousins had been collecting since they were old enough to earn an allowance. Superman, Batman, Green Hornet, Incredible Hulk, Spiderman, who we liked because his real name was Peter Parker. We'd scoop them up and carry them abreast to the living room where, snug up under the blinking tree, we'd spread out and fall into our respective superheroed worlds. Our cousins would man the record player, spinning whatever was new. We shared their tastes: Blind Faith, Derek and the Dominos, *Fresh Cream*, Band of Gypsys, *Live at Leeds, Abraxas, Cheap Thrills.* Sometimes Stuart, the youngest brother, would want to hear some Christmas music. But Clapton prevailed. Clapton was God—I'd read it on a wall near State College. He provided the soundtrack to the endless boxes of overblown, elliptical dialogue and superhuman feat.

I suppose I could lapse here into analytical mode and posit that our consumption of endless tales of superpowers on Christmas morning, accompanied by the hymns of our generation, was a form of worship. But if I thought at all during that anxious hour before we were called to card tables set up in the den and during the harried feast of turkey, ham, rice and gravy, green beans greasy with side meat, broccoli and cheese casserole, fat buttery Jane Parker rolls from the A&P, jello salad, and pound cake; if, afterward, stuffed, back in the living room reading away the quiet hours of early afternoon, serenaded by both sides of *The History of Eric Clapton,* my mind strayed from the comic at hand, it was to dream of Shelly Phillips.

Everything I did on Christmas Day in 1972 I could as easily have done on a Tuesday in July, which is why this year was so different. I'd passed from that point where Christmas was highly anticipated, something to count down days toward, to where it was merely a day when I could not see my squeeze and, as consolation, got to lie around and be rude to my cousins and read comic books and listen to Clapton until the sun began to set over the bare fields bordering the highly inferior hamlet of Saint Paul's and my father went from room to room snatching comic books from fierce clutches and finally, in a last-ditch attempt to get us in the car, picking up needles from records in mid early-seventies-endless-drum-solo. Good-bye, cousins, see y'all next time. In the car we'd miss the comic books. The obligatory fight over which radio station to tune in to (my mother and father, preferring quiet on the ride home, would quell this spat) would make us miss also the albums our cousins spun for our listening pleasure.

My bleak mood was exacerbated by the dire combination of the Back Way as viewed from the Very Back. The light didn't so much die as leak away over the fields. I was stuffed still from lunch, but starving. My sister was all up into my space. To distract myself I would think about Shelly Phillips, and that would work for a while, but I seemed to understand that Shelly Phillips would not last, that everything would change.

Everything changed. My Uncle Bill built a large, sunny modern house on his family farm a couple miles outside of town. Shelly Phillips got tired of my mess. When a few years later my cousins grew up and left home, my aunt threw out most of their comic book collection, which was worth a small fortune then and would by now be enough for early retirement. Clapton went solo and instead of copying the dusty licks of black bluesmen went to ripping off the talented but little known genius J. J. Cale.

Perhaps the most significant change was my attitude toward Christmas, which thereafter arrived with a looming melancholy, for my expectations of its magic, left over from our catechismed and Sears-cataloged childhoods, seemed impossible to meet. I no longer tried. My mind was not on family—surely the cornerstone of Christmases Past—but on Shelly Phillips and the girls who followed her (none of whom, by the way, ever gave me a 45 by King Floyd, or they'd get their own essay). Christmas music began to work my nerves. In its place I listened to the same albums I played the day before and the day after. The whole season thrummed with a low-level but decidedly adult anxiety about how I was supposed to feel. Losing Santa Claus was not such a big deal, but so soon after that Shelly Phillips got tired of my mess, and then it wasn't very long until, morphing into his unappealingly soft-rock alter ego *Slowhand,* Clapton bolted too.

Old Christmas

by Stephen Marion

Before the big snow, three boys Marcus was in jail with got baptized. The preacher was Brother Eric.

I have baptized a many a man in the jails, said Brother Eric.

Marcus looked at him. How about girls? he asked.

I have baptized women in the jails too. Not as many. There are not as many women as men in the jails.

I wisht it was a girl today, said Marcus.

No girls today, young man! said Brother Eric, who had a woolly beard. No sir. None whatsoever.

They were out behind the jail on the dirt basketball court which still had its mostly flat ball on the ground. It was a warm winter day. The air was so warm and quiet Marcus had rolled the sleeves of his jumpsuit all the way up to his shoulders and Brother Eric had taken off his jacket. They had four sawhorses in place and Brother Eric was throwing his blue tarpaulin over them and making his baptismal pool. Marcus saw that Brother Eric had a jailhouse tattoo of a dagger on one arm. Brother Eric never stopped smiling. He smiled all the time as if the sun were hitting his face at an almost painful angle. His smile came through the big woolly beard.

You know what today is, Brother Marcus? he asked.

What? said Marcus.

Today is Old Christmas. I bet you don't know what Old Christmas Day is, do you, Marcus?

Can't say as I do, said Marcus.

Brother Eric was smoothing out his tarpaulin. Would you care to hazard a guess? he said.

They can't be but one Christmas, said Marcus, and we done had that.

Oh, but you are wrong, said Brother Eric. A long time ago they started having Christmas on this day, and then they changed it. You see, nobody really knows when our Lord was really borned. We just know for certain that he was, and what he come for, and that is all that matters.

Marcus tried not to act like it, but he was confused. He had always assumed that these things were more certain. He had always figured that if he ever would ask, some things could be told to him that were fact. But now he looked around. The size of the world on the warm winter day filled him with desire and sadness, as if he had forgotten it. Anyway, it was a good thing this day had come along. The three boys in solitary had about bugged everybody to death about being baptized. They were all charged with murder. Murderers were a different species entirely. Brother Eric had been coming every Sunday, and it got worse and worse about them wanting to be baptized, but the sheriff said he wasn't approving no baptizing in the middle of winter because then there would be earaches and probably pneumonia and damn if the county was paying for that. The murderers about starved themselves. All they would do was lie there and read their New Testaments. The New Testaments were little blue ones that Brother Eric had given them.

I am sorry, Brother Eric told the sheriff. Things like this happens when it gets into mens' souls.

Marcus uncoiled the hose. He was looking forward to smelling the baptism water. Nothing smelled better than the smell of water set free in the air. Marcus wasn't going to say anything right now, because he had his own private ideas about God, and he didn't want Brother Eric to spoil them. One of Marcus's ideas was that God smelled like water. That was what was wrong with religion, he figured. Everybody knew who God was, but when they started talking about him he turned into something else, something that was not God at all. Men were such fools, thought Marcus. They didn't even know when Jesus was born. Marcus watched Brother Eric turn on the hose. I could run, he thought. He liked thinking that he could, but deciding not to.

Okay! Brother Eric hollered.

The hose hissed and lurched and the water came out. Marcus started filling the pool. Brother Eric came up. Works good, don't it? he said.

I reckon, said Marcus.

Are you saved, Marcus? Brother Eric asked.

Marcus didn't say anything. He kept filling the pool.

There is going to be a wonderful place, said Brother Eric. Marcus could feel the shine of his smile. I want you to be there with me.

What do you want me for? said Marcus. I'm in jail.

Brother Eric had lit a cigarette. Really in a way, he said through cigarette tightened lips, I'm in jail too. We all are.

Not like I am.

No. Brother Eric laughed. Somehow he managed to smile even as he smoked. Not exactly like you are. But this old world is a jail.

Marcus looked around.

You don't see the bars, but it is, Marcus. It's like we all got into something we wasn't supposed to get into, and now we are all in the house.

What did you do?

What did I not do, Marcus? That is the question. What did I not do?

I didn't do nothing, said Marcus. All I done was steal a typewriter.

Brother Eric smiled at him as if he were seeing something he remembered fondly in himself. The back door buzzed and opened, and here came the three murderers. They had on shackles and handcuffs, so they were shuffling and jingling, and one of them, the one with a beard, paused a second and looked around and blinked as if he hadn't been in the world in a long, long time.

Good morning! said Brother Eric to the murderers. He smiled down on them as they drew near. It is a wonderful morning, ain't it?

Brother Eric held a long prayer. Marcus didn't close his eyes or bow his head. He looked around. Mull, the jailer, didn't pray either. He was looking straight at Marcus. The murderers had their hands folded and trembling. They had fingers like potato roots.

Marcus and Mull had to lift each one into the pool. Marcus didn't want to touch them. They smelled like gerbils. The first one they lifted, the smaller one without a beard, said, Oh, oh, oh, when they put him in the water, and he shook all over and went on. Brother Eric had put on fishing waders over his clothes. He climbed in and raised one hand and clamped shut the murderer's nose with the other. I baptize you, he said, in the name of the Father, the Son, and the Holy Ghost. He dipped the murderer backward and brought him up, wheezing and coughing and blowing snot.

He was heavier to get out. Then Marcus and Mull put the other two in, one at a time, and Brother Eric did the same thing. After they had lifted them out Brother Eric stayed in and looked around. Is they anyone else this morning, he said, that would like to accept Jesus Christ as Lord and Savior?

It was quiet.

A beautiful warm morning in the middle of the worst winter in a hundred years, said Brother Eric. You might not ever have this chance again. I'd call it a miracle. And I tell you it ain't the only miracle a-waiting on you if you make this one little step.

Marcus stepped forward and climbed in. He was already wet anyhow. Mull didn't even flinch about it. Brother Eric didn't either. He didn't say a word. He just turned Marcus around and raised his hand again toward the sky, which was the palest blue and white.

Contributors

Lynne Barrett received her master of fine arts in creative writing at the University of North Carolina–Greensboro. She is the author of two books of short stories, *The Land of Go* and *The Secret Names of Women,* and coeditor of the anthology *Birth: A Literary Companion.* Lynne wrote the libretto for the children's opera *Cricketina* and has received both an Edgar Award for best mystery short story and a National Endowment for the Arts fellowship in literature. Her stories have appeared in *Tampa Review,* the *Carolina Quarterly, Redbook,* and *Ellery Queen Mystery Magazine* as well as the anthologies *Mondo Barbie, Simply the Best Mysteries,* and *Literature: Reading and Responding to Fiction, Poetry, Drama, and the Essay.* She teaches in the M.F.A. program at Florida International University and lives in Miami.

Rick Bass is the author of twenty-one books of fiction and nonfiction, including most recently a novel, *The Diezmo.* A native of Fort Worth, Texas, he lives with his wife and daughters in northwest Montana, where he is active with a number of environmental organizations seeking wilderness protection for the last roadless areas in the national forests.

Fred Chappell, a former poet laureate of North Carolina, was born in Canton, North Carolina, and educated at Duke University. He is book columnist for the *Raleigh News and Observer.* Among the many literary prizes he has won are the Sir Walter Raleigh Prize in 1973, Yale University's

Bollingen Prize in poetry in 1985, the literary award from the National Academy of Arts and Letters in 1968, and the Best Foreign Book Prize from Academie Française in 1972. He is the author of fourteen books of poetry, two books of short stories, eight novels, and two books of criticism. He lives with his wife, Susan, in Greensboro, North Carolina, where he retired from a distinguished teaching career at the University of North Carolina–Greensboro.

Ellen Gilchrist, a native of Vicksburg, Mississippi, and a graduate of Millsaps College, has published poetry, short stories, novels, and journals. Her second volume of short stories, *Victory Over Japan*, won the National Book Award in 1984. Other awards include the Mississippi Arts Festival Poetry Award, the *New York Quarterly* award for poetry, a National Endowment for the Arts grant, a *Prairie Schooner* award, the Mississippi Academy of Arts and Sciences award, the Saxifrage Prize, the American Book Award, the University of Arkansas Fulbright Award, and a Mississippi Institute of Arts and Letters award for literature. Her most recent works are *The Writing Life* and *I, Rhoda Manning, Go Hunting with My Daddy and Other Stories*. She currently lives in Fayetteville, Arkansas, and Ocean Springs, Mississippi.

Marianne Gingher is the author of a novel, *Bobby Rex's Greatest Hit*, which was made into the NBC Movie-of-the-Week *Just My Imagination* in 1992. She has written dozens of stories which have appeared in a variety of periodicals such as the *Southern Review, Redbook, Seventeen*, and the *Washington Post Magazine*. Some of the stories were collected in her book

Teen Angel and Other Stories of Wayward Love. Her most recent book, *A Girl's Life,* won a *ForeWord* magazine award for best memoir. She teaches at the University of North Carolina–Chapel Hill, where she was formerly director of the creative writing program.

Aaron Gwyn grew up on a farm in central Oklahoma. He received his Ph.D. from the University of Denver and now teaches fiction writing at the University of North Carolina–Charlotte. His collection of stories, *Dog on the Cross,* was published in 2004, and he is currently at work on a novel. His stories have appeared in *New Stories from the South, Glimmer Train,* the *Texas Review, Black Warrior Review,* and various other journals.

Bret Anthony Johnston grew up in south Texas. He holds an M.F.A. from the Iowa Writers' Workshop, and he teaches creative writing at California State University–San Bernardino. His stories have appeared in such places as the *Paris Review* and *New Stories from the South: The Year's Best* (2003, 2004, 2005). The recipient of the James Michener Fellowship and the Christopher Isherwood Fellowship, he is the author of *Corpus Christi: Stories,* in which this story appears. He can be reached on the Web at www.bretanthonyjohnston.com.

Stephen Marion is a native of east Tennessee, where he works as a newspaper reporter. His novel, *Hollow Ground,* was published in 2002. He is also the recipient of a National Endowment for the Arts fellowship in fiction.

Charline R. McCord, a resident of Clinton, Mississippi, was born in Hattiesburg and grew up in Laurel, Mississippi, and Jackson, Tennessee. She holds a Ph.D. in English from the University of Southern Mississippi and bachelor's and master's degrees in English from Mississippi College, where she won the Bellamann Award for Creative Writing and edited the literary magazine. She is Deputy Director for Communications/ Associate Director for CSAP/PIRE's Southeast Center for the Application of Prevention Technologies (SECAPT). She has published poetry, short fiction, interviews, book reviews, and feature articles; coedited *Christmas in the South*, *A Very Southern Christmas*; and contributed to and coedited *Christmas Stories from Mississippi*.

Michael Parker was born in Siler City, North Carolina, and grew up in Clinton, North Carolina. He earned a bachelor's degree from UNC–Chapel Hill and an M.F.A. from the University of Virginia. He is the author of three novels: *Hello Down There, Towns Without Rivers,* and *Virginia Lovers,* as well as a collection of stories and novellas, *The Geographical Cure.* He has published fiction and nonfiction in various journals, including *Five Points,* the *Georgia Review,* the *Oxford American, Shenandoah, Black Warrior Review,* and the *Carolina Quarterly,* and has received fellowships in fiction from the North Carolina Arts Council and the National Endowment for the Arts. His work has been anthologized in *Pushcart Prize, New Stories from the South,* and *The O. Henry Prize Stories.* A new novel, *If You Want Me to Stay,* is forthcoming in fall 2005. Since 1992, he has taught in the M.F.A. writing program at the University of North Carolina–Greensboro.

George Singleton was raised in Greenwood and now lives in Dacusville, South Carolina. He has published over a hundred short stories in magazines and literary journals such as the *Atlantic Monthly, Harper's Magazine,* the *Georgia Review,* the *Kenyon Review, Zoetrope, Glimmer Train,* and six editions of *New Stories from the South.* He is the author of three volumes of short stories: *These People Are Us, The Half-Mammals of Dixie,* and *Why Dogs Chase Cars.* His novel *Novel* was published in 2005.

Judy H. Tucker, a sixth-generation Mississippian, is a freelance writer, a playwright, and a frequent book reviewer in Jackson, Mississippi. She contributed to and coedited *Christmas Stories from Mississippi,* and co-edited *A Very Southern Christmas* and *Christmas in the South.* This is her sixth collaboration with artist Wyatt Waters.

Wyatt Waters was born in Brookhaven, Mississippi, grew up in Florence, Mississippi, and moved to Clinton, Mississippi, in the tenth grade. He holds bachelor's and master's degrees in art from Mississippi College, where he won the Bellamann Award for Art and Creative Writing. Waters frequently teaches art classes in the Jackson area and has had solo shows at the Mississippi Museum of Art and the Lauren Rogers Museum of Art in Laurel. He has published three books of his paintings, *Another Coat of Paint, Painting Home,* and *An Oxford Sketchbook,* and has illustrated *Christmas Stories from Mississippi, A Southern Palette, A Very Southern Christmas,* and *Christmas in the South.* He was commissioned to do commemorative posters for Jackson's Jubilee! Jam, the Crossroads Film Festival, and Washington, D.C.'s Mississippi on the Mall. His work has been featured in numerous magazines, including *American Artist, Watercolor, Art and Antiques,* and *Mississippi Magazine,* and he was the recipient of the Visual Artist Award from the Mississippi Institute of Arts and Letters in 2004. His gallery is located on Jefferson Street in Olde Towne Clinton. His work is also available for viewing at www.wyattwaters.com.

Bailey White was born in Thomasville, Georgia, in 1950 and still lives in the house in which she grew up. She is the daughter of a writer, Robb White, III, and a farmer, Rosalie Mason White. White received her B.A. from Florida State University and became a first grade teacher in Thomasville, a job she has held for over twenty years. Her books include *Quite a Year for Plums, Sleeping at the Starlite Motel,* and *Mama Makes Up Her Mind and Other Dangers of Southern Living.* White's witty comments on daily life can be heard on National Public Radio's *All Things Considered.*

Steve Yarbrough is the author of three books of short stories and three novels, the most recent of which is *Prisoners of War.* A native of Indianola, Mississippi, he teaches at California State University–Fresno, and spends almost every summer in Krakow.

Acknowledgments

IF WE HAD ASKED Wyatt Waters to illustrate this section, he would surely have painted great stacks of colorful books held aloft by literally hundreds of helping hands. That has been our experience for yet another year, being supported by friends, family, and co-workers. As we count our blessings, we wish first to express deep gratitude to Kathy Pories, our editor at Algonquin, who continues to direct us with flawless insight and seasoned experience. We pay tribute to her enormous talent and recognize and appreciate our good fortune to be guided by her bright star. We again thank our publisher, Elisabeth Scharlatt, for her continued support of this endeavor, and we gratefully acknowledge Shannon Ravenel and Lee Smith for the impetus they gave to the birth of this project.

Here at home in Jackson, Mississippi, we will forever be in the debt of the magnanimous John Evans, his second in command, Thomas Miller, and the entire Lemuria crew, who continue to assist us in remarkable and uncountable ways. They smilingly heave and heft our books and regale us with abundant good cheer during marathon book signings. We realize how truly fortunate we are to have the vital support of a strong, independent bookstore right in our own hometown.

Through three books we have been sustained by the abiding presence and support of a nucleus of folks who are year-round gifts to us. These include the people who inhabit the places in our hearts, our families and long-time, steadfast friends—Carolyn Haines, Charlotte Carlton, Peggy Jones, Chris Gilmer, David Creel—folks we depend on for encouragement, advice, and endless favors. We issue a special thanks to the talented Peggy Jones, who delighted us by creating miniature book ornaments—ornaments that gave new meaning to the word "precious"— to decorate not only our trees but the trees of many of our friends. Also, many thanks go to Cheri McHugh and Jeannine Richey for aid, comfort, and counsel and to Harold and Mary Light for their special hospitality.

We thank Wyatt for once again lending his unique vision and talent to this project, and we issue warm and heartfelt thanks to Vicki Waters for her enthusiastic collaboration.

We express our deep gratitude to Fred Chappell for a preface of profound beauty and to the eleven writers represented in this collection. Their writings cut through the bark of the season and expose the encrypted rings that speak of who we are as people, and just how various our lives can be. It is always a spiritual experience to engage the genuine in writing.

Again, we salute the employees of Brunini, Grantham, Grower & Hewes; Union Planters Bank; Adams and Reese; and other great patrons of the arts, who embrace and support the union of fine literature and fine art.